Last Call

Susan Jennings was sprawled on the floor, her half-emptied wineglass on the vanity.

"That's what you get for drinking too much too soon at your own wedding and being so awful to my friend," Nikki said.

A wicked thought crossed her mind. Maybe she should leave the drunken wench to sleep off her self-induced high. She could tell everyone that Susan was passed out and wouldn't be joining the party. That would be pretty rotten, though.

Nikki lightly tapped Susan's face. Something was wrong. Susan wasn't moving at all. Nikki watched for her chest to rise and fall. No movement. Then she bent over to hear her breathing. Nothing. Finally, she took the bride's pulse, her own pulse quickening and adrenaline pumping through her.

Nikki dropped Susan's limp hand as a scream caught in the back of her throat. Susan Jennings Waltman wouldn't be making a formal entrance to her wedding reception, or any type of entrance ever again.

The bride was dead.

Berkley Prime Crime Books
by Michele Scott

MURDER UNCORKED
MURDER BY THE GLASS

Murder
by the Glass

MICHELE SCOTT

BERKLEY PRIME CRIME, NEW YORK

THE BERKLEY PUBLISHING GROUP
Published by the Penguin Group
Penguin Group (USA) Inc.
375 Hudson Street, New York, New York 10014, USA
Penguin Group (Canada), 90 Eglinton Avenue East, Suite 700, Toronto, Ontario M4P 2Y3, Canada
(a division of Pearson Penguin Canada Inc.)
Penguin Books Ltd., 80 Strand, London WC2R 0RL, England
Penguin Group Ireland, 25 St. Stephen's Green, Dublin 2, Ireland (a division of Penguin Books Ltd.)
Penguin Group (Australia), 250 Camberwell Road, Camberwell, Victoria 3124, Australia
(a division of Pearson Australia Group Pty. Ltd.)
Penguin Books India Pvt. Ltd., 11 Community Centre, Panchsheel Park, New Delhi—110 017, India
Penguin Group (NZ), Cnr. Airborne and Rosedale Roads, Albany, Auckland 1310, New Zealand
(a division of Pearson New Zealand Ltd.)
Penguin Books (South Africa) (Pty.) Ltd., 24 Sturdee Avenue, Rosebank, Johannesburg 2196,
South Africa

Penguin Books Ltd., Registered Offices: 80 Strand, London WC2R 0RL, England

This is a work of fiction. Names, characters, places, and incidents either are the product of the author's imagination or are used fictitiously, and any resemblance to actual persons, living or dead, business establishments, events, or locales is entirely coincidental. The publisher does not have any control over and does not assume any responsibility for author or third-party websites or their content.

PUBLISHER'S NOTE: The recipes contained in this book are to be followed exactly as written. The publisher is not responsible for your specific health or allergy needs that may require medical supervision. The publisher is not responsible for any adverse reactions to the recipes contained in this book.

MURDER BY THE GLASS

A Berkley Prime Crime Book / published by arrangement with the author

PRINTING HISTORY
Berkley Prime Crime mass-market edition / June 2006

Copyright © 2006 by Michele Scott.
Cover art by Cathy Gendron. Cover design by Rita Frangie.
Interior text design by Stacy Irwin.

ISBN: 0-425-21021-9

BERKLEY® PRIME CRIME
Berkley Prime Crime Books are published by The Berkley Publishing Group,
a division of Penguin Group (USA) Inc.,
375 Hudson Street, New York, New York 10014.
The name BERKLEY PRIME CRIME and the BERKLEY PRIME CRIME design
are trademarks belonging to Penguin Group (USA) Inc.

PRINTED IN THE UNITED STATES OF AMERICA

10 9 8 7 6 5 4 3 2 1

To Hillarie.
You are loved!

Acknowledgements

I want to thank and recognize Sue Vosseller, Michael Perry, Theresa Meyers, and Rose Kapsner for their help in bringing this book to life. I especially want to thank Lieutenant Brian E. Davis with the Santa Rosa Police department for all of his police procedural information, Monica and Seyamack Kouretchian for their support, Brandi Spracklin for keeping me on the T. Robb track, Quelene Slattery for all of her contributing knowledge about wine, and Colby Arrington who goes above and beyond to keep me organized and is a good friend. A special thank you goes to my personal Yoda, Mike Sirota, who is always there for me, even in a crunch. Thanks to my dear friend Karen Macinerney who is an awesome critique partner and great author. I also want to thank my agent Jessica Faust and my editor Samantha Mandor. You are both wonderful to work with! And, as always, thanks to my best friend and husband, John, and my children Alex, Anthony, and Kaitlin. Live your dreams and live them with passion!

Chapter 1

Nikki Sands took her friend's hands into her own and squeezed, so sorry for Isabel's pain. Isabel had just discovered that the man she'd been seeing and thought she was in love with was not only in love with another woman, but was marrying her.

Worse than that, Isabel had agreed to cater their wedding.

The bride, Susan Jennings, had come to see Isabel only two weeks earlier, claiming that she'd had a falling out with the chef at Domaine Chandon, the caterer she had initially hired. She'd told Isabel that she'd heard wonderful things about her new restaurant, Grapes, and wanted her to take the job.

"I didn't know," Isabel sobbed. She took her hands out of Nikki's to wipe her tears. "I said to that woman that I would do the wedding on such short notice, because I knew it would be good publicity for the restaurant. I didn't know until today, when Susan came into Grapes with Kristof to sign the final contract, that he was her groom," Isabel said in her Spanish accent and blinked back more tears from her dark brown eyes. "I wanted to cry so badly right there, but I could not. I held it back. The worst part was, he acted like he did not know me. Not at all. Like he had never even seen me. I had no idea." Isabel choked on the emotion.

"How could you know? Sonoma is only thirty minutes away but it feels like it's halfway across the world. It's no wonder Kristof was able to fool you. Unless you're in one of those inner circles, you wouldn't have much chance of knowing." Nikki poured Isabel another glass of pinot noir. "You couldn't know." Nikki thought about her boss Derek Malveaux, knowing that he walked within that circle, but he didn't seem comfortable doing it.

Isabel nodded. "Why would he want to marry her?"

When Isabel spoke, she typically did so with her hands as well as her voice. And, when upset, as she was now, Isabel's arms flailed wildly. To Nikki, it said something about the passionate nature of Isabel's Spanish heritage.

"She's mean and nasty and she is not a very nice person," she said. "Ever since that day when I said yes to do that reception, she has called me over all little details. Susan Jennings *es una bruja*."

"I know she's a witch," Nikki replied, understanding Isabel's Spanish. "Who knows why people choose the people that they do." Nikki had met Susan Jennings a few times at various winery events and she wasn't impressed with the realtor to the San Francisco elite. However, her realty work appeared to be helping Susan blend quite nicely with the upper echelon. Those whose trust funds, paychecks or inheritances came with a minimum of six zeroes behind whatever numeral stood out in front.

"Kristof never said anything about being engaged or that he had a girlfriend. If I had known who she was when she came into my restaurant, I would never have agreed to cater the wedding. I would never have signed the contract." Isabel picked up a piece of Ahi Poke she'd prepared for her visit to Nikki's.

"Just call her and tell her that you can't do it, that something else came up, something you have to take care of on that day," Nikki replied. "She can find someone else. It isn't like the Waltmans don't have enough money to find someone else to cater the wedding."

Isabel shook her head. "I can not do that. The wedding is only a week away, and I will not go back on my word. My family is an honorable one. You know this. You have met my brother, Andrés. We are proud. I have also signed a written contract. This deed is done."

Nikki felt a flush of shame and embarrassment. She knew better than to suggest that Isabel Fernandez back out of a signed catering agreement for the wedding of the decade in Sonoma. The heat in her face also signified another reason for Nikki's embarrassment, which came along with the flutter in her stomach with the mention of Isabel's brother's name. There were two men in Napa Valley who'd been able to give her that twinge—one of them was Andrés Fernandez, the other was her boss, Derek Malveaux.

It had been six months since meeting Andrés, Derek, and subsequently Isabel. Time had slid by like time usually does, faster than expected. It boggled her mind that half a year had passed since she had interviewed with Derek Malveaux. One Thursday night last November, she was waiting tables to subsidize her floundering acting career. The following morning, she found herself on board the Malveaux private plane, at Derek's behest, to interview over the weekend for the winery's managerial position. The weekend turned ugly when Nikki found the Estate's winemaker Gabriel Asanti murdered. For a time she'd considered Andrés a suspect, but thankfully she discovered he didn't have a murderous thought behind his hooded dark eyes. At the time, she'd also thought that Isabel and Andrés were an item, until Andrés set her straight by telling her they lived under the same roof because she was his sister.

Isabel was correct; her family maintained pride and a strong sense of graciousness. The Fernandez innate graciousness lent itself to Andrés' edgy good looks. He conjured up an image of Spanish bullfighter combined with bad-boy movie star. A plus to all of that was he knew exactly how to make Nikki laugh.

It didn't take long before Isabel and Nikki started hanging out together and began a close friendship, even though there was a seven year difference in their ages, with Isabel the younger of the two. The two of them had discovered common ground between them. They were the new girls in Napa Valley, and thus carried an air of intrigue about them that captured the interest of many of the Napa Valley natives.

"I hate them. I hate them both," Isabel sputtered and gulped back a large swig of the pinot noir. "But I will not let them harm me any further. I may hate Susan Jennings and Kristof Waltman, but I will cater their damn wedding. And I will do it spectacularly." And having said that, the Spanish beauty laid her head down on Nikki's wooden plank table and cried the rest of her night's tears before passing out. Nikki picked up the emptied plate of sashimi and went to get a bottle of water. Wine limitations were definitely at maximum capacity. Her head whirled and she noticed the slight sway to her step.

She came back to see the shattered, but now unconscious face of her friend, and knew exactly how Isabel felt. With the gentleness of a best friend, Nikki pushed strands of black hair out of Isabel's face and tucked them behind her ears. "I know, girlfriend, unrequited love is a real bitch."

Derek Malveaux and his sky blue–colored eyes passed through her mind before she entertained any further fantasy about him, knowing that her feelings for him were hers only and that his flirting and sweet nature toward her was as simple as that, flirting and nothing more.

She looked back down at Isabel. "Let's tuck you in." It took all of Nikki's strength to lift Isabel onto her sofa, which, good thing for her, stood only a few feet away. Damn, weren't those Firm videos supposed to be giving her some more muscle? She'd even started using the eight-pound weights now. But at thirty-three, okay thirty-five, nothing seemed as easy as it had seven years ago, and having to hide back-fat was now an issue that had recently cropped up. Yep, twenty-eight was a good age. No low-carb diets, no worries about crow's feet, and definitely no back-fat.

She covered Isabel up with a quilt her Aunt Cara sent her from Paris. It seemed that since her aunt's retirement from the Los Angeles police department as a homicide detective, Aunt Cara had discovered a new life in Europe. What was supposed to have been a month-long backpacking trip through Western Europe had now turned into something more. Aunt Cara had been gone for as long as had Nikki from Los Angeles. Nikki suspected a man might be involved in keeping the woman who'd raised her away, across a whole lotta land and even one really large ocean. Eventually she'd get over there and find out just what was going on with Aunt Cara.

Her friend sound asleep from wine and a broken heart, Nikki stepped out of her cottage. It had originally been the Estate guest cottage, but since her arrival, she'd unintentionally taken it over. It just happened that way. Derek put it out there when offering her the job and it truly was icing on the cake with her decision to go to work for the winery. Nikki's mind running amok with thoughts of Isabel's predicament,

she decided to take a walk around the vineyard and over to
the pond, one of her favorite places at Malveaux Estate for
its calming effect. Hopefully, Ollie would be outside and get
a whiff of her scent and come along. Ollie, the vineyard
Rhodesian Ridgeback, belonged to Derek, but since Nikki's
arrival amongst the vines, the dog spent quite a bit of time
with her, causing some lighthearted chiding on her end toward Derek, whom she knew was a wee bit jealous that
man's best friend had divided his loyalties.

She glanced around. No Ollie in sight. Bummer. The
cold air sent a shiver through her and helped to sober her.
But the chill faded fast with her pace and she almost forgot
all about it, taking in the evening smells and sounds that
the spring brings to the wine country. A bullfrog croaked in
the distance keeping time with the chirp of crickets, creating their own nature's concert. The night's breeze picked
up the scents of Mexican orange blossoms and star magno-
lia, blowing them across the vineyard, creating a fragrance
no perfumer could re-create.

The pond came into view, a light on over at Derek's place
illuminated through the Spanish moss dangling off the old
oaks, shedding a glimmer on the water's edge. Derek didn't
live up in the Estate mansion because his stepmonster lived
there, and on occasion his half brother Simon and his lover
Marco, who were now off in New York doing the spring
fashion shows, with Marco presenting his new line. The
stepmonster, Patrice, knew her way around the country's
best spas and lately had been kept busy frequenting them
more than the vineyard, which suited Nikki just fine. She
knew Derek wasn't exactly upset over Patrice's absences.
Of course, Simon and Marco, whom Nikki liked to refer to
as the Boys of Summer, with their spray on tans and white-
on-white attire, weren't missed either.

The breeze blew into a wind, chilling Nikki's face. She

rubbed her hands together. Was that the Cowboy Junkies version of "Blue Moon" she heard coming from Derek's house? Getting closer, she determined it was, and sat down on a log next to the pond to take it all in.

Her eyes closed, and lost in thought, she was startled by a rough tongue licking her hand. She jumped and her eyes flew open and she laughed out loud to see that she'd been found. "Hey Ollie, I was hoping you'd make it." She patted the big dog on top of his reddish-colored head. He wagged his tail in delight and continued licking her hand.

"What about me?"

Nikki spun around on the log, nearly tearing her sweatpants. There stood Derek. Strong, blue-eyed, tanned, blond, rakish Derek. "Oh, hi. I didn't know you were there, too." Why was it that every time she opened her mouth to say something to him, she sounded like either a blubbering little girl or a total idiot?

"Yep." He sat down beside her. "You glad to see me, too?"

"Sure I am."

"I gave you a call earlier to see if you wanted to have a glass of wine with me. Thought maybe we could barbeque some steaks. I guess the butcher didn't hear me correctly when I ordered my meat today. He gave me too much. I would have liked to have had you join me. But I got your answering machine, and when I walked on over to your place, I saw Andrés' car parked out front. I figured you were busy."

"Really?" She smiled. This might be interesting to play out for a minute. "I turned my machine down and didn't answer it because I was busy."

"Obviously." He looked away from her.

Okay, she was going to tell him the truth, but it sure made it a helluva lot more fun to take a different path in getting there. "I had a nice wine tonight."

"Did you? I suppose it was one of Spaniard's Crest's," he said, mentioning by name the winery Andrés made wines for.

"Actually, no. It was a Sonoma wine. I know, call me a traitor, but it was damn good."

He laughed. "Please. You know me; I think we should drink wines from all over, not just here in Napa or from this vineyard. Although we do make the best." He grinned at her.

"Going to be quite a wedding next week in Sonoma over at the Waltman Estate." Nikki shifted on the log, and fiddled with the silver bangle bracelet decorating her wrist. Another one of Aunt Cara's gifts from Europe.

"Apparently so. I've been contemplating going. I suppose I have to. I sent in my reply card awhile back."

"It should be a good time." If she didn't know better she would've sworn he mumbled something about how much fun could a wedding be, going alone. "What? Did you say something?"

"No." Derek picked up a stick and tossed it out across the pond for Ollie who leaped to his feet and charged for the prize. "How's Andrés?"

"I suppose he's fine. The last time I saw him, he seemed good."

"Didn't you see him tonight?"

She stifled a smile. "Actually no. Isabel is over. In fact, she's staying the night. We shared a couple of bottles of wine and she drank a wee bit more than me. She's had a rough week."

"Isn't that Andrés' jeep in front of your place?"

She nodded. "Isabel needed it because her car is in the body shop. Remember? I told you that someone backed into her in the parking lot at Grapes."

"That's right, you did." He snapped his finger and pointed at her. He sighed. Ollie came bounding back and dropped the stick at his feet. He tossed it again. This time the stick landed in the middle of the pond and Ollie, with all of his enthusiasm, dove into the water. They both laughed, and the tension between them floated out into the air. "You know, I've known Kristof Waltman and his family forever, and even though I'm not too keen on weddings, it would be disrespectful of me not to go."

"Yes, that's probably true."

"But I don't really want to go alone." Ollie flew out of the water and came up to them, shaking pond water all over both of them.

"Ollie," Nikki hollered. Not that she was wearing her best outfit, but that cold water sent a chill through her white knit sweater and to her flesh, causing it to prickle. She slapped her arms in front of her, but the look on Derek's face said that he might have seen just how cold she was.

"You crazy dog," Derek said, and took off his sweatshirt, handing it to Nikki. It was hard not to notice that he wore a tight T-shirt underneath that flattered his abs, and pecs, and biceps, all of those areas that could make a woman weak in the knees. "Put this on. I'll walk you back to your place."

They made it to her porch and she started to take off the sweatshirt.

"Give it back to me tomorrow."

"Thanks. I'd invite you in for tea or hot chocolate, but Isabel . . ."

"I understand. You better get inside and warm up."

"Right." She started to open her front door, when Derek caught her arm.

"I almost forgot with the dog getting us all wet and everything." He glanced around. Ollie looked up at him expectantly. "But uh, I don't really want to go alone to the wedding. Would you like to come with me?"

Nikki felt her lips move, she was certain her brain registered and the vocal chords worked, but what she said sounded inaudible to her. Like a distant echo and as if it came from someone else's voice, but she knew she'd said "yes" as she closed the door behind Derek, forgetting what she'd told Isabel earlier that evening about unrequited love.

Ahi Poke with Kenwood's Reserve Sauvignon Blanc

When the blues hit, and that man you thought was the man of all men disappoints, call up your best pal, get together, and make up some yummy Ahi Poke. Not only is it tasty, it also treats that waistline gently so that the next time you see the fool, you'll be five pounds thinner and a helluva lot smarter for hanging with a friend whom you can always count on to drown your sorrows with. Nikki would recommend drowning those sorrows with a bottle of Sauvignon Blanc. One to try is Kenwood's Reserve Sauvignon Blanc. This delicious white is fruity, with peach, vanilla, and a touch of grass.

Eat like it's buffet style and drink the good white. You'll forget the loser in no time.

Ahi Poke is a Hawaiian treat. You'll find it at most Luaus. Everyone has their own version. This one is easy and not as traditional, simply for the ease of it as some of the traditional ingredients can be difficult to come by.

Serves 2–3 (depending on how big the eaters or
how brokenhearted those involved are)
1 lb sashimi-grade yellowfin ahi or aku
1 tbsp chopped red onion
1 tbsp chives
Juice squeezed from one lime
1 tsp crushed garlic
Sesame oil to taste (anywhere from 1–2 tbsp)
1 tsp sesame seeds
1 tbsp teriyaki or, for less of a sweet flavor, use soy
sauce

Cut ahi into small cubes. Blend all the ingredients together and refrigerate. Give it at least an hour. This is a fun recipe to scoop into martini glasses and eat as an appetizer or first course.

Now if you do not like raw fish, you can still use this recipe. Instead of eating it raw, sautée it as your main dish. Let the marinade sit for an hour and then heat pan with olive oil, toss in the ahi mixture when hot, and while continuously mixing, cook for 3–5 minutes, depending on how you like your fish. Ahi is meant to be at least pink inside. If you make the recipe this way, you will not need to purchase sashimi-grade ahi. Grill grade will do just fine.

Chapter 2

Nikki grabbed Isabel's arm from across the bar counter as Kristof Waltman's bride-to-be's cackling turned heads inside the restaurant. The very thin, very long-legged Susan Jennings sauntered into the quaint but swanky new place in town. Her wavy pale blonde locks swung with her every step. The friend at her side worked the room with her. Both of the women possessed ivory skin of perfection. However, the future bride was the light pale one with ice-green eyes, while her friend sported dark brunette waves and brown eyes.

"It's almost as good as watching Paris Hilton and Nicole Richie slinking on in," Nikki said. "That is, if they were still slinking together."

The patrons eating lunch at Grapes, located in Yountville, couldn't take their eyes off what could only be classified as the spectacle of Susan Jennings, soon to be Susan Waltman, and her counterpart, Pamela Leiland, a one-time Victoria's Secret model.

Nikki had come by to eat lunch and more important, to check on Isabel, knowing that she'd be doing last-minute preparations for tomorrow's big event. It looked like she'd made a wise decision. Isabel needed as much moral support as she could get because, as Nikki suspected, her friend was a wreck. Moments before the boobsy twins arrived, Isabel had gone into the kitchen to order a turkey burger with sweet and spicy jalapeño sauce for Nikki. To add to the support system, Nikki took it upon herself to call Andrés and insist he come down to the restaurant and comfort his younger sibling. He still hadn't arrived when Susan and Pamela showed up.

The hostess seated the two women at a table on the patio. It didn't take long before Susan Jennings was requesting to speak with Isabel.

Nikki winked at her. "Don't let it or her get to you. Kristof Waltman doesn't deserve someone as sweet as you. Keep your guard up out there with her. She's a barracuda."

Isabel nodded, pulled her petite frame to its full stature of five feet, two inches and headed to the patio. Nikki spotted an open table close by, between the open glass partition and the patio. She could easily move and probably overhear their conversation without them knowing. A protective urge for her friend took over. If Isabel needed some assistance, then she'd have to jump in. Maybe scratch Susan's eyes out. This could get dangerous.

Nikki took her Diet Coke and moved to the table. Sure enough, as she expected, Susan's perfectly lined and painted lips were moving a mile a minute before Nikki even sat down.

"Here's the problem that you're not understanding, Isabel. Marty, Kristof's father, doesn't care for mushrooms.

So, although I know the mushroom dumplings I sampled are absolutely divine, like all of your food, we just can't have them." Susan shook her head vehemently. "Can not, can not have them. Okay? Let's get on the same page here."

"Ms. Jennings, they are only one of several selections of appetizers. Not everyone care for the mushrooms, so that is why I suggest to you, the sampler plate you choose."

Nikki knew that when Isabel grew nervous she had a more difficult time than normal with the English language, and she could tell her friend was struggling.

"I *understand* that, but you see, my future father-in-law has generously put in quite a bit of money for this event, and it's important we do the right thing by him."

Nikki shifted in her chair. She'd met Marty Waltman and he didn't strike her as the pompous, finicky type. Did Susan know about Isabel and Kristof? Was this a power trip for her? Or was it simply her way, to be mean and abusive to people she obviously considered beneath her? Nikki cringed, because she knew exactly how it felt to be Isabel at that moment.

Susan carried on as the waiter set down Nikki's burger. "I'd like oysters of some type. I think they would be such a nice addition, considering it is a wedding, and you know oysters are supposed to be an aphrodisiac."

Nikki choked on her burger, and took a swig of her soda.

Isabel visibly shifted her weight from one foot to the other. "Ms. Jennings, it would be impossible to find that many oysters for a wedding reception of five hundred people at a late hour such as this." She smiled sweetly at her.

Nikki felt for her, but she was doing a good job dealing with the bitch.

"We have no more than a day," Isabel continued. "I do not think that if I called all of my contacts in San Francisco they could do this. You must understand. Someone would have to package them and drive them the sixty miles out here, and then I would still have to make preparations for them. It would be quite a difficult task." Isabel crossed her arms in front of her.

"Susan, she's right. Try to be reasonable here," Pamela interrupted.

"Fine. Fine. So no oysters. But no mushrooms either." She wagged a finger at her. "Isabel, you need to come up with an alternative. Charge more, or whatever you need to do. Why don't you work something up for me and give me the price difference while we eat our lunches. Present it to me before we leave. And, we are in a bit of a hurry. I have to check with the florist still, and then get my nails and hair done for the rehearsal dinner and festivities. It's good that you're only doing the reception, and not tonight's dinner. I'm not sure you could handle them both."

Isabel remained cool and patient, keeping a smile on her face the entire time. Nikki knew her friend had to be boiling inside, because she was about to get up herself and go all prizefighter on Susan Jennings.

Isabel turned to walk into the interior of the restaurant, and as if on cue, Susan called after her. "By the way, Isabel, in case you would like to take our order, I need you to bring us a bottle of your best champagne. This is all about celebrating, isn't it? We'll start with the Gorgonzola and endive salad. The one with the strawberry balsamic vinaigrette. Leave out any garlic though. I don't want any bad breath. I do have a groom to kiss."

Isabel turned back toward the table and nodded. "I will be right back."

Nikki saw Isabel bite the corner of her lip as she walked back into the restaurant and headed to the kitchen without even glancing her way. Lo and behold, with impeccable timing, Nikki also noticed a disheveled but gorgeous Andrés enter the restaurant at that moment. His gray T-shirt with a dirt smudge across the front of it made him that much more endearing. By the looks of him, she'd reached him while he was out in the vineyard. He spotted Nikki first and came over to her table, and sitting down across from her, he asked, "What's the problem?" She nodded her head in Susan's direction. "Oh, no. Has that woman been bothering my sister again?"

"You could say that," Nikki replied.

"I don't understand her. Isabel has worked hard to pull this wedding off for her and she keeps coming back for more and more changes. She's a bitch."

"I'll second that."

"What I really don't understand, is why Isabel allows her to get to her so. That's not her usual way. My sister has never been one to let anyone boss her around, not even our mother." Andrés made the sign of the cross against his chest. "My baby sister is a fighter. You've seen her pull this restaurant off and make a name for her business in a short time, even though she's an outsider. Why Isabel would let that nasty woman get to her is beyond me. It's not at all like her."

Andrés didn't know about Isabel and Kristof's fling. Nikki read it in his eyes and could tell by his words. Had he known about Kristof and Isabel, he would've understood completely why his sister reacted the way she did to Susan. Furthermore, Nikki found herself convinced that Susan Jennings did indeed know about what had occurred between her fiancé and Isabel.

"I don't know either, Andrés." It wasn't her place to tell Isabel's brother about his sister's relationships. "What I do know is that Susan Jennings does get to your sister, or at least her unrealistic expectations and harassments do, and she needs your support right now."

"Where is she?"

"In the back, retrieving a bottle of champagne for them."

He stood. "Thank you." He took Nikki's hand and kissed it.

Soft, powerful lips. Wow. Nice. Very, very nice. Nikki did like the romance and affectations that came along with Andrés Fernandez. It was his way. She'd known when he sat down across from her moments before that at some point he would make the exact gesture he'd just made. She'd anticipated it because every time they met it was the same. He was indeed a lady's man, although completely unintentionally. It came naturally to Andrés. She watched him walk back to the kitchen and then bring out the champagne for the ladies on the patio.

"Ladies," he said in his Spanish accent. "I believe this is for you. I'm Andrés Fernandez, and I've heard all about your pending nuptials, Ms. Jennings. I wanted to come over and congratulate you myself."

Both women's eyes rested on the man before them. Nikki laughed, because she knew that even with the dirt smudged across his shirt that he'd shut down Susan Jennings with his charm and good looks. Pamela Leiland batted her long lashes at him and Nikki thought she might lose her lunch for the second time that afternoon.

Isabel came out and sat down across from Nikki. "You did not have to call my brother. I am a big girl, you know."

"I'm sorry. I thought some big-brother support was what you needed."

Isabel smiled. "Thank you. I suppose he is what I need right now, as you are, too. You are a good friend."

"Looks like he's tamed her for the moment. What are you going to do about the change she wants?"

"You heard all of that?" Nikki nodded. "I am crossing my fingers she will be willing to do a simple prosciutto wrap with balsamic dipping oil. It does nicely to pair it with the champagne like the other appetizers and it is easy. And, as a Spaniard, I have to ask you how many people dislike thin ham slices wrapped around green beans and Parmesan? If this country is like my own, then the ham will be a good choice. Every street corner in Madrid has a *tienda de jamón.* A ham store."

"Sounds like a winner. Ham does notoriously well here, too, especially at feasts, which it sounds like this event will be."

"Indeed." Isabel stood up as Andrés walked back inside. "I am going to get this over with."

"I took their order. I'll deal with it," he told her, walking on past them.

Isabel watched her brother take the order back to the kitchen. "He is too good to me. I know he has much work to do at the winery, but he is right here helping me." Her eyes brimmed with tears.

"That's what family is for," Nikki replied. She thought about her own family back in the hills of Tennessee. None of them would ever be there for her, not in the way that Isabel and Andrés were for each other. The only way any of her numerous siblings or her mother might even show up is if they found out that Nikki was doing pretty well for herself. The only one of her family who was ever there for her was her aunt, and she was now thousands of miles away. She sighed heavily and wiped any remnants of lunch from the corners of her lips with her napkin.

"Want to try my new cheesecake?" Isabel asked before going over to Susan and Pamela's table.

"Yes, but no."

"Please. It is delicious and it would make me feel pleased if you would try it."

How could she resist a plea like that? "You're terrible,

Isabel. But for you, I'll do it. But you know, I can't say that my hips and thighs are going to like you anymore after this."

"Oh baby, it is not your body I'm after. I love you for your mind."

"Good thing, because my body is going to cellulite city at this rate. First a burger and now cheesecake. You'll be the end of ever seeing me again in a bikini."

"Maybe, but you will never feel denied and that is what is most important."

After finishing her cheesecake, which was as delicious as Isabel promised, Nikki noticed that Susan and Pamela appeared to be done with their lunches. She kept her eye on her pal and the enemy as Isabel presented her solution to Susan whose face went taut. "I suppose that'll be fine. If you'll excuse me, I have to go to the restroom. Can you just add our lunch check to my reception bill?"

"Certainly," Isabel replied.

Andrés came back out of the kitchen with a slice of cheesecake for himself and sat down across from Nikki. "It looked too *delicioso* to pass up," he said, pointing to her now-emptied dessert plate. "You look good, too."

"Thanks." Nikki knew the red was rising in her face, because her ears burned and when they burned it usually meant that her face matched them shade for shade.

"You do. I like that color of shirt on you. It matches the green in your eyes. Did you lighten your hair or something?"

"I did." She'd visited the hairdresser only days earlier to try and return to the "natural" blonde highlights, which had faded as of late. Her once golden hair color had turned a shade too close to caramel, or more accurately, dirty blonde/mousy brown. "I trimmed it up too." It now skimmed the top of her shoulders and was cut in a wispy fringe around her face to frame it. The stylist's exact words were *flirty* and *sexy*. That sounded good.

"It looks very pretty. I hear you're going to the wedding with Derek. Isabel mentioned it."

"I am."

"Nice. I'll be there, too, helping out Isabel with the wines and cooking. All of that. She's going to need it. I'm hoping that all the staff shows up on time. I can't imagine anyone needing to have so many people at a wedding. I wouldn't find that special. It is more like a production. I'd rather have something more intimate, a few friends. *Romantica*. That would be the way I would want it."

"I know what you mean." Nikki crossed and uncrossed her legs underneath the table.

Susan broke the repartee between Andrés and Nikki, as her heels clicked upon Grape's adobe tile floor, on her way to the restroom. Nikki turned to see Pamela handing Isabel a handful of cash and overheard her say, "I'll take care of lunch. There's no need to add it on to the reception bill. I'm sorry she's behaving so badly. Pre-wedding jitters, I think."

Isabel thanked her. As Pamela and Susan left, Isabel pulled up a third chair at the table and sank into it. "Lunch is over. The real work starts now. I am not opening for dinner tonight. I have so much to do for tomorrow's preparations."

"Do you need help?" Nikki asked.

"No. I have a large staff arriving in about an hour. I have been doing work all week to get everything ready. I think I will be all right."

"If you need me, you know where to find me."

Nikki started to stand as Andrés held up his hand, got out of his chair and went around to hers, holding it out for her. He gave her a kiss on each cheek. She turned and hugged Isabel, then waved over her shoulder as she left.

Getting behind the wheel of her silver Camry, Nikki saw Susan whip out in front of another car in her BMW 760.

The driver, in a family wagon with a carload of kids, had to slam on the brakes, skidding as she did, frantically honking her horn at Susan. Nikki gasped and shook her head. Par for the course with this woman. She reflected on the way Susan treated Isabel, and it appeared to be that way with anyone who walked across her path. It did seem increasingly clear that Susan Jennings had a knack for making enemies.

Jalapeño Burger with Ravenswood Merlot Sangiacomo

When it comes to making a good turkey burger, it's all about adding seasonings. There isn't a better choice than jalapeño to turn up the heat, especially if you have a handsome Spaniard seated across from you. Then again, you probably wouldn't need any spice—but sans hottie bullfighter, chop up the jalapeño and mix yourself up one tasty lunch. If it's a middle of the week thing and you find you have to go back to work or take care of some little people, (you know, the kind who don't think you have a life, other than serving them—that's right, your children), then imbibing probably isn't an option. Hell, maybe it is. However, if it's say, a football Sunday or a rainy Saturday when you might want to pop in a Gipsy Kings' CD and curl up with a good book, then, by all means open yourself a bottle of Ravenswood Merlot Sangiacomo. This wine is a delicious blend of summer fruits and earth flavors. It has a full, ripe flavor quality, making it a nice balance with dark plum, cherries, blackberries, tobacco, and spice. This wine will be even better with a year of aging. It's bold enough for the burger and with a hint of sweetness, a delicious blend with the spicy jalapeño flavor.

    2 lbs ground beef or turkey
    Salt and pepper
    Bleu or feta cheese
    4 hamburger buns

Tomato slices, onion slices, and lettuce as
    accompaniment
1 clove garlic
¼ cup olive oil
½ cup chopped jalapeño peppers
½ cup yellow onion
½ cup chopped cilantro
½ cup balsamic vinegar
2 tbsp Worcestershire sauce
1½ cups sugar. You can supplement Splenda for a
    lower cal dish; however, read the sugar versus
    Splenda sweetness conversion on the label for
    accurate amounts
2½ cups water
Salt

Heat the olive oil in a large saucepan to medium-high. Sauté
the peppers, onion and garlic until soft. Add the vinegar,
sugar, Worcestershire sauce and water, and bring to a boil.
Decrease the heat until the mixture is thick and syrupy,
about 30 minutes. Season with salt. Let cool, then transfer to
a bowl, add the cilantro, and refrigerate until ready to use.

Season the meat with salt and pepper and shape into 4
patties. Cook on the grill or pan. During the last minute or so
of cooking, top the meat with the cheese to allow it to melt.

To serve, place each patty on the bottom halves of the
buns and spoon over pepper mixture, then top with accompaniments. Serve immediately.

Gorgonzola and Fresh Greens Salad with Strawberry Balsamic Dressing served with Gloria Ferrer Blanc de Noirs

Now if you're into the Gucci and Prada scene and all about making a statement with your best gal pal, then forget the burger dish and mix yourself up a chichi salad. The Gorgonzola cheese with endive lettuce and strawberry balsamic vinaigrette is an excellent fit with Gloria Ferrer's Blanc de Noirs. This champagne is a full-flavored berry delight. It showcases a mouthwatering blend of black cherry, strawberry, and raspberry flavors. The pretty pink color of the champagne makes it perfect to serve at bridal showers or a ladies' lunch. The color comes from a special pressing technique that extracts an extra measure of color from the grapes harvested by hand. This wine also has a touch of spice that enhances the flavors of the Gorgonzola in the salad. This is totally an all-girls lunch dish, no guys allowed, because it wouldn't fill them up and they'd think it too pretentious anyway. It's perfect for a gossipy good time. Annie Lennox would be the diva to have crooning in the background for this get-together.

1 head romaine or any type of lettuce you prefer.
Or, to make it easy, pick up one of those salad bags of mixed greens.
½ cup walnuts (you can candy these if you prefer by using 1 tbsp of butter and 2 tbsp brown sugar. Melt butter in a pan, toss in chopped nuts

and brown sugar, cook until sugar bubbles and
caramelizes, take nuts out, let them cool and
then break them apart to toss into salad.

½ cup of crumbled Gorgonzola cheese.

½ cup of strawberries (optional), also—any berry
will do as well as a blend—blackberry &
raspberry, etc., be as creative as you like.

Dressing

¼ cup extra virgin olive oil
¼ cup balsamic vinegar
2 tbsp strawberry preserves (you can use sugar free
   if you like)
Black pepper to taste

Blend dressing ingredients in a Cuisinart or blender. Mix
salad ingredients together, drizzle with dressing. Serves 4.

Chapter 3

Nikki combined a yawn with a groan while waking on Saturday morning. Anxiety-filled dreams had kept her tossing and turning through the night. She couldn't help the combined sense of dread and anticipation planting itself squarely in her gut. Maybe today would be a tell-all day. She was actually going to a wedding with Derek. Couldn't that be considered a date? At least a borderline one? He hadn't made it sound like a real date with his excuse of "not wanting to go alone," but a girl could dream.

She clambered out of bed and pulled on her morning attire of exercise pants and T-shirt. Time to put fantasies aside. She headed out on her daily run down to Yountville where she could grab a cup of coffee and check up on Isabel.

Something about stepping out onto fertile ground bright and early always livened her senses. She couldn't help but appreciate where life had taken her in recent months. A long way from the glitz of Hollywood and even farther from the back hills of Tennessee.

Her feet pounded against the dirt road that led down to Highway 29, as she took in the imagery of rolling green hills surrounding her, mixed in with various golden hues of sienna, burnt oranges, and rich browns.

She reached Yountville and deviated from her usual routine of grabbing her cup of joe at the Bouchon Bakery with its scrumptious flaky croissants and gourmet coffees, because she knew Isabel would be at Grapes preparing for the reception, and could probably use a helping hand. Sure enough, a line of delivery trucks, their metal doors rolled up, were filling up with tray upon tray of food. A steady stream of workers Isabel had hired for the event continued bringing it on.

Nikki rounded the front door and came face to face with a harried Isabel shouting orders, her fingers pointing in all directions.

She grabbed Isabel gently by the shoulders. "Hey, hey. Slow down for a minute, Izzy B," she said. "They all look like they're doing the best they can. You don't want to get a reputation for being difficult. I know this thing is tough on you, but let's look at it as an opportunity. You pull this off and do the job I know you will, everyone in the wine country and beyond will know you and want you for their events."

Isabel nodded, her eyes watering. "I know. I am being stupid. I have been stupid all along. I thought I loved Kristof though, you know? Crazy. It is not like he ever told me that he loved me. We did not spend much time together as my mind thinks about it. I understand why now. I thought he was busy with the vineyard and winery, but he was spending time with his bride-to-be. I was what you call here in America, an extracurricular activity. A fling."

"Forget Kristof Waltman. He's a jerk. Once the day is done, you can move on. I'm gonna grab a cup of coffee and then you're going to put me to work. Deal?"

"No. You have a busy day yourself. You *are* going with Derek tonight."

"What does that mean?" Nikki took a step back.

"It is exactly that. If you want to make me tell you what I mean . . ." She shrugged. "I will say that he is handsome, he is nice, and *you* have a sweetness for him."

"I do not. I'm too old for crushes. He's my boss and friend. He needs a date he can go with and not feel pressured by. This isn't a real date."

"Nikki, you do not convince me. I do not think you convince yourself." Isabel winked at her. "The cafe is in the kitchen and if you want to help, I suppose I will not turn you down. And because you made the point yourself—it is not a real date with your *employer*."

They both giggled and Isabel went back to giving orders, only this time she brought her barking down a notch.

Nikki knew that if she admitted it she did have feelings for her boss. And, she hoped that his invitation to this wedding was an indicator that he reciprocated those same feelings. They'd forged a connection right after she'd decided to come to work for him and she'd saved his life from a murderer who had killed his friend, and the Malveaux Estate's winemaker, Gabriel Asanti. And, even though they flirted and she thought there was something between them, neither one had pursued it. Maybe that would all change tonight with the two of them going to the wedding together.

Thankfully, the day passed by in fast motion. Before long mid-afternoon was upon them, and Isabel wanted to grab a quick shower before heading over to the Waltman Estate to oversee the event.

Andrés showed up during the preparations and helped

out through the day, too. Nikki hadn't gotten a chance to really talk to him much because they'd all been so busy.

The work done at Grapes, and the food on its way to the Estate, Andrés came over to Nikki and draped an arm around her shoulder. "I'll give you a ride home, since it's getting late. I know you have to get ready for tonight."

"Yeah, I suppose showing up in a T-shirt and jogging pants wouldn't work, huh?"

"If anyone could pull it off, it's you. Come on, let's go."

"You are good for my ego."

A strange silence sat between them once in the car. Andrés turned on the radio. Stephen Stills was singing "Love the One You're With." Nikki crossed her legs and rolled her head from side to side, hearing her neck crack. Why the tension? She was with one of her best friends, and there had never been anything awkward between them before. Andrés hummed along with Stills. Nikki cracked her window.

Andrés never brought anyone with him to the various parties they'd attended. Neither had she, for that matter. He'd never mentioned a woman, but a man like Andrés must've had many loves. She'd never asked, but maybe there was a woman back in his native Spain or in Argentina where he'd gone to the university to study viticulture. Although she was curious and wanted to ask him about it, a larger part of her didn't.

Neither of them said anything during the five-minute ride back to the Malveaux Estate other than it had already been a long day and they both felt for Isabel and the night ahead she'd have to endure. Andrés pulled up in front of Nikki's place. "Have fun tonight."

"Thanks, and thanks again for the ride. I'm sure I'll see you at some point in the evening. You're still going to help Isabel, aren't you?" she asked.

"Of course. I'll probably see you." He leaned across the seat and gave her an awkward kiss on the cheek.

She shut the door of his truck and turned to wave upon reaching her porch. He waved back. When had things gotten tense between them? Was there something more going on there than she'd recognized? Sure, they flirted and he was a wonderful man, but her sights were always really on Derek. Maybe they shouldn't be. Why was she thinking like this? She'd never thought about marriage or family too much before. Since leaving Los Angeles where it was cool to be single and carefree and coming to Napa, it had become increasingly difficult not to notice the families that lived here and the ties that bound them. A white picket fence, Prince Charming, and two children might not be such a bad thing.

An hour and a half later she remembered exactly why her sights were set on Derek as he looked ridiculously too good to be true, his eyes matching a medium-blue silk shirt and navy pinstriped suit. His blond hair, naturally highlighted from all the time he spent in the sun on his land, emphasized his golden tan. He stood in her entry and for a moment she couldn't speak.

"Wow," he said. "You look . . . Wow."

"Thanks. It's a little something I picked up at one of the boutiques." What a lie that one was—a little something. Right, a little something that cost a quarter of her two-week paycheck. The sea-green silk dress made her look big busted. And she kind of liked *the look*. Hey, there was no fooling around on this *not real* date. She was going vavavoom all the way.

They took off in Derek's Range Rover and made the windy pass to Sonoma. After half an hour of driving, they pulled into the wrought-iron gates at the Waltman Castle, which looked like a true gothic blast from the past. What a setting. There wasn't a car on the lot that had cost less than $80,000. The valets were dressed in velvet knickers, white tights and top hats.

"Over the top," Derek said.

"Something tells me we haven't seen anything yet," she replied.

He laughed, nodded his head and threaded his arm through hers.

It was a costume party of haute couture as the women had donned their Gallianos, Guccis, Pradas, and Armanis. The men wore the gamut from expensive suits to tuxes. Nikki glanced at Derek walking beside her.

"What?" he asked, obviously feeling her gaze.

"I'm just wondering what you might look like in a tux."

He rolled his eyes. "I don't do monkey suits, sweetheart."

"Oh, a rough and tough macho type. I see now. I'm figuring you all out, Derek Malveaux."

"Good. When you have me *all* figured out, could you fill me in? I'm not Mr. Machismo. I don't like the idea of a tux; hell, I fought with myself over putting on this suit."

"It's true, your usual attire are those jeans you love and a T-shirt, but I have to say that you don't look half bad in that suit. I kind of like this new look for you."

"Don't get used to it," he teased.

They continued to walk up the brick pathway toward the Waltman Mansion, replete with turrets, steeple tops, and built from the ground up with a dark-grey brick. There was something almost frightening about the place. No one could deny its beauty, but Nikki wasn't sure she'd want to live here. Some of the rumors she'd heard around town maintained that the place had a resident ghost. By the looks of it, she wouldn't doubt it.

"Do you believe the story about Old Man Waltman?"

Nikki referred to Kristof Waltman's great, great grandfather and the original owner of the Waltman Estate and vineyard. He'd built the empire. The Waltmans were five-generation Sonoma farmers, although it was doubtful that Kristof did any farming at any point. Maybe his dad Marty took a turn among the vines now and then, but from what she knew of Kristof he was *too busy* with extracurricular activities to be working in the trenches.

"The ghost story? That he roams the castle at night? That's a tale. A fun one, but no, I don't believe it."

"You don't believe the story? Or you don't believe in ghosts?"

"I'll never say never, but until I see one, I have my doubts."

They walked up the front steps, and the back of Nikki's dress caught on her heel. She started to fall, but Derek grabbed her before she hit the ground.

"Are you okay?" He held her in his arms.

"I, uh. Yeah. Jeez, I feel like a total klutz." She faced him.

"Let's get inside and make sure you're alright."

"It's no big deal. I'll be fine. I'm glad I didn't tear the dress." She laughed it off, but for what the dress cost her, she meant it.

They started to walk again and she realized she needed to be concerned with more than a twist to her ankle. She'd broken the damn strap on her sandal.

The mansion inside had mahogany hardwood floors, wrought-iron spiral staircases, and walls painted a golden color, illuminated by candlelight. Nikki suggested to Derek she take a minute to go upstairs to the restroom. Most of the people were already milling toward the outside to get their seats. Susan obviously liked purple because it abounded throughout in all shades. The flowers of choice—Sterling

Silver roses with their soft lavender color and deep floral
smell permeated throughout. Magenta-colored lilies tucked
in between the roses snaked through the banisters. The lilies
had also been placed in tall crystal vases. The candles lighting the castle were a deep, dark, almost black purple.

Nikki walked on her aching foot, trying not to limp up
the stairs. At the top she found a massive hallway going to
the right and another to the left. Not seeing any directions,
she went to the right. Walking down the hall she saw the
groom's dressing room. A little ways farther was the bride's
room.

There stood Susan Jennings outside the room, all Vera
Wanged out in silk and tulle in a dress that had a vintage
thirties feel to it—beaded down to the ground, thin straps
on the shoulder leading into a plunging neckline, and cut
on the bias. Her golden hair waved into what could only remind someone of a Marlene Dietrich look, from the era of
black and white movies. Susan gave the word *stunning* a
new meaning with the kind of glamour of days gone by.
Another woman stood with her, hands on hips, wearing a
low-cut black-sequined number and a smirk on her face.

Nikki overheard her saying to Susan, "It's only right
that you should ask your only sister to be in the wedding. I
can't believe that you didn't ask me. Am I that much of an
embarrassment to you?"

"Jennifer, I don't have time for this. Go and take your
seat, please. I've done plenty for you. Beyond what any
other sister would do. How fast you forget what I *have* done
for you. I can change that, too, if you want to keep up the
moaning and groaning." Susan heard Nikki's footsteps and
looked over at her. "What do you need?" she asked curtly.

"Actually, the bathroom."

"You were supposed to go down the other hall. Didn't
you see the signs?"

"There weren't any."

"You've got to be kidding? I told the help to put out signs for people. I swear, if you want something done right, apparently you have to do it yourself. Fine." She let out an aggrieved sigh. "There's another one a few feet down that way." Susan pointed behind her.

Endless halls, dozens of bathrooms and bedrooms, a person could get downright lost for a couple of years in this place.

"Hey, wait," Susan called out after her. "Aren't you Isabel's friend? Shouldn't you be in the kitchen?"

"I'm a guest. I'm here with Derek Malveaux."

Susan raised her eyebrows into a comical arch. "You're working your way up the ladder. Impressive. A girl after my own heart."

"That's for sure," said Jennifer, the woman whom Nikki presumed to be Susan's sister. Susan gave her a dirty look.

Nikki found the restroom. However, curiosity—one of her traits that usually got her into trouble—got the best of her as she whipped around, once inside the bathroom, and cracked the door to see if she could hear anything further between the two squabbling siblings. She couldn't hear them very well, but she could see that they were both heated up. She leaned closer into the crack of the door. What she saw next surprised her. Susan Jennings opened her small beaded purse and handed Jennifer what looked to be a check. Wasn't it supposed to be the other way around on wedding days? The bride and groom receiving monies and gifts?

Jennifer looked down at the check. "I thought it would be more."

"God, leave me alone and get the hell out of my way. I'm going to get married now. Go sit down, Jennifer, and stop being so damn greedy."

Susan went back into her dressing room, slamming the door behind her. "You'll pay more. I doubt you want Kristof knowing all your dirty little secrets," Jennifer said to the door, and then in a huff walked toward the stairs.

Nikki did a quick fix on her high-heeled sandals, knowing that if anyone attending the wedding saw them they'd be aghast at the spectacle her right foot was now strapped into, but there wasn't much else she could do.

On her pained foot, she found herself behind Susan's entourage of bridesmaids and a flower girl, with Pamela Leiland holding up Susan's lengthy train. They, too, had that long ago–era look going for them, but all in the various shades of purple, with the flower girl wearing the lightest of lavenders on up to Pamela, whose beaded number was the darkest of the dresses in that almost purply black. None of them took note of Nikki, who knew she better find Derek quickly.

Once down the steps, the bridal party went out the side door and as Nikki turned to go the other way toward where the guests were seated, someone tapped her on the shoulder. "Excuse me," a young man in a courier uniform said. "Do you know Sara Waltman?"

"I know who she is," Nikki replied.

"Good. Can you see that she gets this?" He handed her a large letter size envelope.

"Sure." She took it and felt a bit awkward for doing so, but she understood the man's need. He had a job to do, and she was all he could find inside the castle at that moment. Nikki signed for the letter. It had Sara's name on it and she would have to remember once the nuptials were over to find Kristof's great aunt to make sure she got the envelope. As she went inside to set the envelope down on the foyer table behind a vase of flowers, she couldn't help noticing the return address. It read "Lawson & Rennert," and then, "San

Francisco Premier Investigative Services." Kind of interesting. Sara must be having someone investigated. Well, this winery and vineyard she was vested in was a multi-million dollar company, and she wasn't getting any younger. It probably had something to do with her will. It really wasn't any of Nikki's business, so she set the envelope behind the vase and made a mental note to tell Sara when she saw her.

It took several more minutes before Nikki found Derek. He'd waited for her over by a gazebo draped in purple velvet and flowers. "I was getting worried," he told her.

"I'm fine." She pulled up the side of her dress to show him the sandal.

"Nice legs."

"My sandal, silly. I had to try and fix my shoe so it'll work for now."

"I knew that. Let's take our seat. The music is starting."

Nikki soon became distracted as the groom and his groomsmen came onto the scene looking dapper in their tuxes. Kristof Waltman was the kind of man you'd take a second look at, with light blue eyes and medium brown hair that he wore slightly longish and wavy. Today he'd slicked it back. He had a baby face look about him and was almost too pretty-looking to be a man. She understood the attraction Isabel had toward him, even though he wasn't Nikki's type at all.

She and Derek were seated toward the front and she couldn't help wondering who the parents of the bride were, because no one looked old enough to be the parents. On Kristof's side were his dad, and Great Aunt Sara, along with several other family members. But no Mom Waltman. Rumors abounded that Mom had left a very young Kristof and Dad behind years ago, for someone with even more money and a desire to spend it, rather than save it like Marty Waltman was known to do. But if he was the one footing the bill for this shindig, he'd spared nothing at all.

Nikki did see Jennifer seated in Susan's family section. Next to her sat a tall, dark man with a Guido-the-pimp look going on. He also appeared kind of pissed off, with his lips down-turned and his eyes reflecting a glint of what Nikki thought might be hatred. She had to wonder what was the source of his anger. Or maybe that was the way he always looked.

Before long the wedding march played and the guests stood for the bride's procession down the aisle. Once up there with her groom, the nuptials didn't take long. Apparently these folks wanted to get to the party, which, lucky for them, and for Nikki's ankle, was only a few feet away.

As soon as the newlyweds walked back down the aisle as Mr. and Mrs. Kristof Waltman, the guests rose to their feet, and within minutes the party began with music echoing off the hills, and the wine flowing freely, along with the appetizers coming by on trays and being passed out to those wanting to have a taste.

Nikki and Derek found their table before getting any wine. She set down her purse and turned to go with him to the bar.

"No. Take a seat. I can tell your foot hurts."

"I'm fine."

"No, you're not. You're ornery. Now take a seat, I'll get us a couple of glasses of wine and some goodies."

She sighed as he walked away. An older gentleman who stuck out his hand soon joined her at the table. "Blake Sorgensen."

She took it and shook, introducing herself. "Nikki Sands."

"Quite an event. It doesn't surprise me though. Marty spares no expense when it comes to Kristof. I've known them for years and Marty is terrible about spoiling that boy, but I can't blame him after his mother left them both the way she did. I would've spoiled a kid, too, if I ever had any children, but I'm a confirmed bachelor."

"Oh. What do you do?" Nikki didn't know enough about Kristof's past to be prying. She decided it best to turn the conversation toward Blake Sorgensen himself. She was sure he'd have no problem with that.

He took out a cigar and lit it, puffing on it till a plume of acrid smoke rose up past his silvered hair. He might've been a handsome man once, but his reddened cheeks and bleary eyes gave her every indication that Blake was a drinker and had been for years. He waved his hand in the smoke trying to get it to blow away from her. Awfully thoughtful.

"A little of this, a little of that. I dabble in all sorts of businesses."

Alrighty then, and that meant what exactly? She was relieved to see Marty Waltman walk up about that time. He slapped Blake on the back. Pamela Leiland was at Marty's side. "Hey there, old man, are you picking on this pretty lady?"

"No. I'm hitting on her and who are you calling old?"

This guy was getting sleazier by the minute. She found it difficult to believe that he and Marty were friends. Marty looked like the kind of man she'd always envisioned she'd want for her dad—calm, clean-cut, usually with a smile on his face. He wore glasses, which gave him a look of intelligence. It must've been good to be Kristof growing up, but then again he hadn't had a mom, and she could relate to that feeling. Sort of. Or at least she knew the feeling of being abandoned by her mother. Besides, she understood better than most that one couldn't judge a book by the cover.

After another minute of small talk, Pamela tugged on Marty's sleeve and they walked away just as Derek returned with the wine and a variety of appetizers. Sitting down, he handed Nikki a glass of chardonnay. They clinked their glasses together in a silent toast and took a sip. He winked at her and she thought she might just melt right on down into the white wine with its smooth melon taste and honey notes.

"Don't you two make a nice couple?" Blake said. "You really do, and for the record, I was only kidding about hitting on you. I've learned my lesson with you younger women. You either love and leave us rich old bastards after spending a bunch of our money, or you wind up wanting a house full of kids. I'm too old for any damn kids. You two are the right age for each other. Marty better watch it with that young thing he's got hanging on him. He'll either wind up burnt or having to remodel his gaming room into a nursery." He nodded in the direction of Marty and Pamela.

Neither Nikki nor Derek knew what to say. She did find it interesting to see Pamela Leiland so tight with the father of the groom. How did Susan feel about that, and more so, what did Kristof think? Pamela was a good thirty years younger than the senior Waltman.

"Will you two excuse me? I hate to take off early from this shindig, but I've got a plane to catch. I bought a yacht down in Cabo recently and I'm headed there for a few days of some R and R," Blake Sorgensen said.

"No problem," Derek replied.

Nikki stifled her laughter as they watched Blake rush over to the bride who was making her rounds through a throng of people. He reached her, drawing her away from the group surrounding her and pulled her close, hugging her quite intimately.

"I thought he was Marty Waltman's friend," Derek commented. "Looks pretty close to the bride, too."

"I think he's fairly toasted already. Too bad he has to go. Nothing like having an obnoxious drunk at the table to keep you entertained." She took a sip from her wine. "I hope he has a driver."

"It's good he's leaving for *Cabo*." Derek emphasized *Cabo* in a haughty tone, feigning to be the pompous Blake Sorgensen. "Anyway, I doubt we would have needed him to entertain us, Nikki."

Ooh, trumped and stumped. No reply for that one. Lucky for Nikki, she didn't need one, as the bride started a bit of commotion.

"Your name is Louis Faulker?" Susan laughed out loud. The crowd around her laughed some, too. A few people walked away. "Like fucker, only Faulker? You poor thing. You really should take that nametag off, Louis. I'm so sorry for you."

A young man in his early twenties blushed, his head down. He wore a tux and was one of the staff Isabel had hired for the evening. He'd been passing out appetizers when Susan had apparently decided it would be fun to tease the poor man. Nikki remembered talking to him briefly earlier at the restaurant while loading the trays. He was slight, already balding at a young age, had bad skin, and wore thick glasses.

"Who hired you?" Susan continued.

Isabel rushed to Louis' side. She whispered something in his ear and he left, going toward the kitchen. Isabel handed Susan a glass of champagne. Nikki noticed Kristof wink at Isabel. She started to stand, wanting to give both King and Queen Slimeball a piece of her mind.

However, the band started to play The Isley Brothers "For The Love Of You," and Derek grabbed her hand. "Wanna dance?"

Nikki turned back to glance at Isabel and the bride. She appeared to have it under control. Derek squeezed her hand. "Sure."

"Foot hurt too badly?"

"Uh, uh." She kicked her sandals off under the table,

not caring who saw. Derek escorted her onto the large section of patio serving as a dance floor. He held her tight and close. He smelled like sweet woods. She closed her eyes. Were his eyes closed? She leaned her head on his chest. His really strong chest. God, he felt good. The song wound down. Did the dance have to end? Her entire body tingled while he twirled the loosened tendrils of wispy hair that had fallen from her chignon on the back of her neck. But the dance did end, with neither one of them quickly pulling away from the other. Until the band started playing the ever-so-popular wedding song—"Love Shack" by the B-52's.

"Thanks," he whispered, grazing her ear with his lips. He held her hand walking back to the table when she remembered Isabel and the spectacle Susan had made prior to the dance.

She didn't even have to tell Derek what she was thinking because he said to her, "Do you want to go and see about Isabel?"

She nodded and told him she'd be right back, because she definitely wanted another dance. She was so elated she even forgot to put her sandals back on and she nearly forgot how much her ankle hurt.

She found Isabel hustling around in the kitchen. "Hey, you okay?"

Isabel handed her a glass of wine. "No. No, I am not. I had to send poor Louis home. I will probably wind up paying for therapy for him. Can you believe that woman?"

Nikki shook her head.

"Do you know what she did now? She came here into the kitchen again, making complaints about my phyllo wraps."

"They were delicious."

"Yes, but not according to *her*. Can you take that up the stairs to her?" Isabel pointed with her hot mitt at the glass of wine she'd handed to Nikki. "She is in her dressing room making a change of clothes into her next gown, for her and her groom to make a formal entrance."

"You've got to be kidding me? I'd say she's already made an entrance and then some."

"Do I look like I am making it up? She wants another glass of wine, and she wants it now. I poured her one minutes ago when she came in to make complaints. She is buzzing the intercom down here for another one, and all of my people are working fast to take care of all the other details."

"No problem. Only a few more hours and this nightmare will be over." Nikki ascended the stairs, feeling terrible that Isabel was having such a hard time.

She tapped on the bridal room door. No answer. Nikki opened the door, not caring if Susan Jennings screamed at her for entering unannounced. But Susan didn't scream at her. Instead, the woman was sprawled out on the floor. Her wineglass half emptied on the vanity.

"That's what you get for drinking too much too soon at your own wedding and being so awful to my friend."

Nikki walked over to her and slipped her arms under Susan's shoulders to try and lift her. "You've got to get up, Queenie, and make your entrance." A wicked thought crossed Nikki's mind. Maybe she should leave the drunken wench to sleep off her self-induced high. She could go out and tell everyone that Susan was passed out and wouldn't be joining the party. That would be pretty rotten. "Listen here, Mrs. Thang, you've got a gazillion guests out there waiting to see you partying some more in all your glory, so get your butt up and get going." Nikki lightly slapped Susan's face. She couldn't have drunk that much booze in such a short amount of time.

Something was wrong. Susan wasn't moving at all. Nikki laid her back down on the floor and watched her chest for a few seconds, watching for it to rise and fall. No movement. Then she bent over to hear for her breathing. Nothing. Finally she took the bride's pulse, her own pulse quickening and adrenaline pumping through her. Nikki dropped Susan's limp hand as a scream caught in the back of her throat, realizing in horror that Susan Jennings Waltman wouldn't be making a formal entrance to her wedding reception. In fact, Susan Jennings Waltman wouldn't be making any type of entrance anywhere ever again. The bride was dead.

Chapter 4

Confused guests, distraught friends, and a tormented bride-groom watched as the coroner's van pulled out of the Walt-man Estate.

Nikki stood next to Derek, whose arm hung protectively around her. "I can't believe it. I really can't believe it." She looked at the people around her, whose faces all reflected that same general feeling of disbelief.

"I know. Poor Kristof. What do you think it was that killed her?" Derek replied.

"I don't know, I mean maybe she was doing some type of drug and along with the alcohol she had a heart attack. But she didn't seem all that bombed when we saw her earlier before she headed into the house."

"No, she didn't. Other than that she was pretty obnoxious with that poor kid passing around the appetizers. I suppose the police will be questioning him," Nikki said.

"I'm sure they'll be questioning all of us."

"Ms. Sands? Are you Nikki Sands?" asked a man's voice from behind her.

She turned around to face what she knew to be one of the detectives who'd arrived on the scene shortly after the uniformed Sheriff's deputies.

"Yes."

He stretched out his hand. "I'm Detective McCall, and I was wondering if you'd come inside the house with me so I can ask you a few questions. You are the one who found the body and phoned in the emergency call. Isn't that correct?"

"Yes."

Detective McCall pulled a sheet of paper from his pocket and read something from it. "Are you Derek Malveaux?" he asked.

"I am."

"Guest list." McCall waved the piece of paper at him. "Good. We'll also need a statement from you. Why don't you both come with me, and I'll have you speak with another one of the detectives."

They both followed the razor-thin man, who was also basketball-player tall with feet to match, into the mansion. His comically high-water pants were offset by his pretty green eyes that said there wasn't anything but brains behind them. He had thick brown hair that fell slightly over his eyes and when he smiled Nikki knew the man had one pride and joy in his life. He'd definitely been to Brite Smile or had worn those bleaching trays or something, because Detective McCall had the whitest teeth Nikki had ever seen, and that was saying something after living in Hollywood for several years. They were also perfectly lined up.

Derek stuck by Nikki as they entered the castle and she could sense his desire to protect her. She couldn't help being a bit old-fashioned at that moment in appreciating his gallantry. Chaos reigned throughout the Waltman Castle grounds shortly after the 911 call she'd made, as news spread quickly about what had happened. Uniformed deputies were the first to show on the scene, followed by the fire department, the plainclothes detectives, and the coroner's office. The sheriff had sectioned people off into groups until the detectives from Santa Rosa, which was the closest city with a detective branch, finished investigating the scene in the changing room and the body was removed. No one was calling this a murder investigation, yet. But the thought hung in the air like the thick fog rolling into the valley. The guests had been there for a couple of hours already, and some were becoming pretty antsy.

As Nikki and Derek entered the castle, they saw Kristof sitting on the bottom step of the spiral staircase, holding his face in the palms of his hands. Marty Waltman held Pamela Leiland in a tight embrace while the maid of honor sobbed.

Tiny, ancient Sara wobbled in from the kitchen with the use of her cane. "I've asked the caterer to brew some tea, sweet boy," she said to Kristof, who looked up at his aunt with a tear-stained face and reddened eyes.

A handful of cops stood in the foyer, comparing notes and defining how the questioning of the guests would proceed.

Marty let go of Pamela long enough to offer a handshake to McCall, who seemed to be in charge of the investigation.

"Mr. Waltman," he replied. "I'm sorry for your tragedy this evening."

Isabel came in with a tray of teacups. Her eyes locked with Kristof's. Nikki noticed that as she set the tray down on a table and poured Kristof a cup her hands shook. Nikki wanted to go to her and comfort her. Regardless of how

Isabel felt toward Susan or even Kristof, she was a good-hearted woman and what had occurred with Susan's death was bound to eat away at her, as it was everyone else. Nikki smiled at her and declined a cup of tea.

"We'd like to ask you and your family a few questions." McCall turned back to face Nikki. "If you could hang on for a second, please."

She nodded.

"Are Miss Jennings, I mean Mrs. Waltman's parents, available?" McCall proceeded.

Kristof looked up at the detective. "Susan was an orphan. Her parents died when she was a teenager. Her only relative is her sister, Jennifer. She's upstairs in the bathroom."

"Okay. We'll need to speak with her. In fact, we'll need to talk with everyone here today. Once we're through with that, people can go ahead and leave. I have a good group with me, so it shouldn't take as long as it might sound."

"Is that really necessary right now?" Marty cut in. "Our family has suffered greatly this evening on a day that was supposed to be a celebration. I'm certain our guests want to leave. It's been a horrid ordeal for everyone. I understand the need for questions. We have them ourselves. However, we'd appreciate some time to absorb what happened. Tomorrow might be a better time for us."

"That's understandable, Mr. Waltman. But the fact that Mrs. Waltman died the way she did leads us to believe that it's a bit suspicious."

"Are you saying that my wife could've been murdered?" Kristof set the cup of tea he'd been sipping on the table next to him and stood up. "That's ludicrous. Everyone loved Susan. She is the sweetest woman I know." He hung his head in realization that speaking about Susan in the present was no longer an option.

Nikki hated the idea of thinking badly about the dead, but Susan *sweet*?

"Do you know if she was using any drugs?" McCall pressed on.

"Gentlemen, that's crazy. Susan was not that type of woman. I knew her very well. She married my son, for heaven's sakes," Marty said.

At that moment a voice from the top of the stairs rang out, "Well, she did like to take a toot of cocaine once in awhile."

All eyes turned upward to see Jennifer standing there, a glass of champagne in hand and her Italian gigolo at her side.

"And who might you be?" McCall asked.

Jennifer descended the stairs and introduced herself. "I'm not saying that she was some kind of party girl, but she knew how to have some fun if the occasion permitted. It wouldn't shock me if she had considered her wedding day one of those special occasions."

"That's ridiculous, Jennifer," Kristof said.

"Then you didn't know her as well as you think you did. Right, Pamela?"

Pamela glared at Jennifer. "Why do you want to be so ugly, Jennifer? Your sister loved you. She's gone and you're dragging her name through the mud."

"Please. Love me? Okay. Whatever. Look, I'm only telling the truth, and you know I am. We've all partied together at one time or another." Jennifer winked at Pamela.

Kristof looked back and forth from Pamela to Jennifer. "Is this true, Pamela?"

McCall held up his hand. "Alright, people, this has been a terrible tragedy, and I again apologize for the loss. However, for now we do have questions and the sooner we get to them, the faster we can proceed." He turned and instructed the other detectives to prevent the groups gathered for questioning from speaking to each other until after their statements had been given. Once finished with directions, the officers spread out like army ants reckoning with the leftovers before them.

McCall escorted Nikki into the family room where he questioned her. Nikki looked back over her shoulder and saw Derek walking away with one of the other detectives.

"When you found her, there was no sign of breathing or a pulse?" McCall asked.

Nikki was seated across from him on a cream sofa. He stood and jotted down notes. She wished he'd sit down. He was pretty intimidating standing there hovering over her in all his skeletal height. "Nothing. I shook her and tried to even pick her up at first thinking that maybe she'd already had too much to drink, but when I realized she wasn't breathing I called the emergency number."

"How was Mrs. Waltman this evening? What was her demeanor like?"

"She seemed a bit stressed out."

"Why would you say that? What exactly was she doing that made her appear stressed out?"

"I don't know. She snapped at some of the servers, and I overheard her have a bit of a run-in with her sister."

This remark raised an eyebrow. McCall pushed Nikki on this, and she told him what she'd seen just before the wedding. He continued to ask her questions about how well she knew Susan and what her link to her was. He asked her if she knew of anyone who might want to harm her or of anyone who had a grudge against her. She simply shrugged. Isabel's face flashed across her mind, but so did several others, so all she told him was that Susan wasn't the nicest or most popular woman in town. At the end of the interview, Nikki asked her own question of the detective. "Do you think that Susan could have been murdered?"

"Right now we have to look at this as a crime scene, until we can conclude it is something else. We won't really know exactly what we're dealing with until we get the autopsy report back on Mrs. Waltman."

"You're going to cut my wife up?" exclaimed Kristof, walking into the room.

"Mr. Waltman, I asked you to remain where you were until I had a chance to speak with you."

"My wife died here tonight, and you want me to sit still until you can get to me? I can't sit still. I can't wait. I want you to find out now what happened to her!" he wailed.

"That's what we're trying to do, Mr. Waltman. Now, please, I'll be with you in a moment."

"You're not going to cut my wife open!" Kristof cried. "You can't do that! I won't let you do that!"

Overhearing his son's raised voice, Marty entered the room, Pamela following behind him. He walked over to Kristof and put a hand on his shoulder. "Son."

"Dad? They can't do that to her. No!" He shook his head emphatically, tears welling in his eyes again.

"I'm sorry, but under the circumstances we have to find the cause of death," McCall said.

There was an edge to the detective's voice that never let up. Nikki couldn't help wondering if he ever got a chance to enjoy life.

"They're right, Kristof," Pamela interrupted. "Don't you want to know anyway? I'm sure it will help put your mind at rest. We need to know. I don't think she was doing drugs, and I'm sure there wasn't foul play involved. It was probably some fluke thing. She might have had some heart problem, something like what John Ritter died of. Something that no one ever knew about. But we really do need to know."

"I can't deal with this right now." Kristof stormed off.

McCall sighed and Nikki heard him say under his breath, "It's going to be one long-ass night." He looked at her and handed her his card. "Thanks for your help. If anything else comes to mind, stop by or give me a call. I may need to speak with you further."

She fished her business card from her small evening bag, making it easier for him in case he did need to contact her.

"I'm going to see about Isabel for a moment," Nikki said, after locating Derek, who had also completed giving his statement.

He nodded. "I'll go to the bathroom and meet you at the car. I was told that once we've given our statements we can go."

"Good."

Nikki went in search of Isabel in the kitchen. The somber mood had carried over to the catering staff, who were now quietly washing and stacking dishes along with wrapping up all of the leftover food, and placing trays back onto trucks. Andrés appeared to have taken charge of the situation. He glanced at Nikki and nodded in the direction of a sitting area just off the kitchen.

She went to Isabel. "Are you okay?" She sat down in a chair opposite her friend.

Isabel nodded. "I . . . No. I do not know. I hurt so bad"—she lowered her voice—"for the things I said the other night. About the way I felt toward Susan and Kristof."

"What you told me was only natural. Any woman would've felt and said the same things. My goodness, Isabel, you were or are in love with Kristof. He was carrying on with you behind his fiancée's back and you weren't even aware that he had a fiancée. He used you, and you're allowed to feel the way you did and do. Susan was awful to you. It's terrible that she died, but she didn't die because of the way you felt about her. You can't put any of that on yourself."

Andrés walked over and put his arm around Isabel. "I put Mary in charge of finishing this up. I'm going to drive you home. You need some rest. I'll come back and make sure it all gets done."

"I should stay. It is my job," Isabel protested.

"Your brother is right. Have you spoken with the police?" Nikki asked both of them. They had.

"Why do you two play parents to me?" Isabel laughed through her tears.

"Because we both know what's good for you," Nikki replied.

"She's right. Now come on. Get your things. Let's go."

Isabel stood and hugged Nikki. Andrés gave Nikki his usual sweet kiss on the cheek and she watched as they left through the kitchen's back door.

Walking back to the front of the castle, Nikki saw that the door to the den was open. She peeked inside the dimly lit room and spotted what looked to be the envelope that had been delivered earlier to Sara Waltman and it appeared to have been opened. In all the commotion someone had found it. The likely candidate would have been Sara herself since it was addressed to her.

She knew she should have better control and should probably push aside her inclination to play Nancy Drew, but she didn't. Instead she snuck into the den and before she could change her mind, she was reaching inside the envelope.

"Oh, no," she said to herself, holding the edge of a black and white photo and quickly thumbing through a handful more.

"Excuse me? Hello?"

Nikki looked up to see Sara standing in the doorway, her eyes squinting as if trying to focus. Nikki shoved the envelope behind her back and inched it back onto the desk, hoping the older woman hadn't noticed that she'd been holding it in her hands. She was grateful that the room was poorly lit, but not so poorly that Nikki didn't know that what she'd seen in those photos was indeed a reason for one or more members of the Waltman clan, or even someone else, to have murdered Susan.

Chapter 5

Nikki had to think fast on her feet and hope the older woman bought her story. "Hi. I was looking for my purse," she said, knowing that Derek had offered to take it with him as he headed out to the car.

"It wouldn't be in here," Sara remarked.

"I realize that now. An attendant took it from me for safekeeping in one of these rooms when we first arrived for the wedding. With everything that happened tonight, I can't remember which room she told me it would be in."

"The coat room, dear. All the coats and purses were to be put into the coat room."

"Of course," Nikki replied, laying a hand on the woman's shoulder. "I can be a bit ditzy sometimes."

"Oh, I doubt that," Sara replied. "You're that young woman who works for Derek Malveaux. The one who helped solve the winemaker's murder some months back.

I recognize you from the papers. Such a brave girl you are."

"Not me. I didn't really solve anything. I really should be going. Sorry to have gotten lost."

"Yes, you have to be careful around this old place. My grandfather walks these halls, you know. I hear him at times. He was a son of a bitch, even worse in death than life as he's always banging around wanting to keep us from sleep since he can't seem to rest in peace himself."

Nikki was startled by Sara's terminology for her grandfather, albeit she couldn't help but be amused by it.

"I've even had a shaman over here to get the old bastard to go to the Light or somewhere but here, but no. He doesn't have my grandmother or mother to torment anymore; because there's no doubt when those two died they got on past him faster than you can say *boo*. No. The old fart wants to drive me crazy because he knows I never liked him and he never liked me. Hell, no one ever liked him! You hear that, Grandpa? You always were a pain in the ass and you still are a pain in the ass!" Sara lifted her cane up in the air, shaking it.

"Gosh. Well." Okay, so what do you say to that? Nikki had no clue, but she was ready to hightail it outta there. Listening to the ranting of a ninety-year-old was not exactly what she wanted to be doing at this point, and she didn't need anyone else walking into the office and seeing her there. She got the feeling that Sara might be old, and even strange, but not stupid. Nikki couldn't help wondering if Sara hadn't seen more of what she had been doing in the den than she'd let on. Nikki knew there was a good possibility that Sara may have seen those pictures herself. Someone had. "I've got to go. Thank you for everything. I am terribly sorry for your loss."

"What loss? I never liked that blonde pickpocket hussy anyway. Good riddance. Maybe if we're lucky she grabbed grandpa on her way out of here and took him to hell with her."

"Right. Good night." Nikki wanted to leave that comment *and* Sara as quickly as possible.

She met Derek at the car and before long they were on their way home.

"You're sure quiet," he said as they drove back over the pass.

"A lot happened tonight." She'd already decided not to say anything to him about the photos she'd found. She knew Derek wasn't crazy about her occasional side job of wine country snoop.

"It did. I'm sorry you found Susan like that. It must've been terrible for you."

"It appears I have some sort of magnet that attracts me straight to dead bodies." She tried to laugh at her own macabre joke, but couldn't.

Neither did Derek. "I really didn't want things to go this way tonight. I wanted us to be able to talk and laugh, dance . . . you know. We're always so focused on our business and since I haven't replaced Gabriel with a new winemaker yet, I've been busy trying to do it myself."

"I know. It's okay."

He sighed. "Do you want to stop off at Hurley's for a late supper? We can catch up. I've missed visiting with you."

Nikki knew what he meant. Since the loss of the Malveaux Estate winemaker shortly after Nikki came to work at the winery, he'd buried himself in his work. Nikki was so new that she'd taken his lead and worked constantly herself, learning everything she could about the wine business. When she'd first started working for him, they'd taken some time to hang out in the evenings and share dinners, while he educated her on winemaking and grape growing. The industry fascinated her and so did Derek Malveaux. But he was always the gentleman and never took it any further than the casual business relationship they shared. However, Nikki knew at least for her, that something was bubbling inside her for Derek and she wished that he felt the same way toward her. She'd realized soon after taking the job at Malveaux that he would need time to get over some of the rough stuff that had gone on in his life in the recent past, including an ugly divorce. And she'd decided he was worth the wait.

"What do you say?"

She wanted to. She really, really wanted to, but she also wanted to sort out in her mind what she'd seen in those pictures inside the envelope at the Waltman Castle. "Tell you what. We're both tired. Why don't you come back to the cottage with me for a nightcap and some snacky stuff? You like *Saturday Night Live*?"

"Let's do it."

Once inside Nikki's cottage she poured them each a glass of chilled pinot noir.

"Look at you," Derek commented when she handed him the glass. "You continue to amaze me."

"What, with chilling the red wine?"

He nodded and took a sip.

"I recently read a small article in one of the wine magazines about which reds taste good chilled. This one topped the list."

"I can see why, with the strawberry and floral notes. I think the chilling enhances it. What do you think that floral note is?"

Nikki brought the glass to her nose and inhaled the bouquet of the wine. "Violet, maybe?"

"I think you're right. I like this idea. Maybe we should see how our zin would taste chilled."

"I think it would be good." Nikki went back to the kitchen and set her wine down on the center isle in the kitchen. Alrighty. She rubbed her hands together and then opened her fridge, finding what she was looking for—a roasted chicken. She roasted at least one a week and made it one of her staples. This one was perfect for what she was about to do because she'd roasted it in an ancho chili rub.

Derek walked over to her and reaching around her set his wine next to hers. Having him so close inside her cottage sent her nerves churning. "Can I help you do anything?"

"Um, sure. Grab a knife if you don't mind peeling and slicing a couple of those mangoes." She pointed to the ripe tropical fruit in a bowl.

He selected three of them and the next thing Nikki knew, Derek was performing a juggling act for her. She opened her mouth and covered her laughter with her hand. "I would've never guessed."

"Yes, it's true, I'm a closet juggler." He dropped one of the ripe mangoes, which went splat on the floor. "Wait, let me change my title, I'm a world-class juggler." They both laughed. Derek set the other two mangoes on the kitchen island. "I think maybe I should stick to winemaking."

"There does seem to be more money in that, and I hate to tell you, but it doesn't appear juggling is going to be your claim to fame." Nikki grabbed a dish towel off the counter and bent down to wipe it up. He bent down too, scraping the fruit into his palm. He looked at her and their laughter subsided.

"Here, let me do that." Taking the towel from her hands he finished wiping up the mess on the floor.

Nikki stood and fanned herself with her hands, then grabbed her glass of wine and took a big gulp. Good thing it was chilled. Derek finished cleaning the mess and started peeling the mangoes. Nikki cut up an avocado and some scallions and then placed the ingredients over some mesclun. "Okay, I'm ready for those mangoes."

"Me, too," he replied and then went suddenly bright red.

Nikki opened the fridge and stuck her head inside to find a lime, figuring her face was as red as his, and not wanting him to see. It was funny how they seemed to always do that with each other. Those double entendres. For goodness' sakes, innocent words should not make a grown man and woman blush.

Nikki squeezed the lime on top of the mangoes, then mixed all of the ingredients together with some oil and balsamic. All in less than ten minutes a fairly healthy gourmet dinner was created.

"Nice night, should we take it outside?" Derek suggested.

"Why not? Let me get my sweater." She went back into her bedroom and slipped out of the spectacular sea green Calvin she'd worn. She pulled on a pair of light blue cashmere sweats Aunt Cara had indulged her with last Christmas, the label on the inside reading Juicy. It made Nikki smile. How could you not feel good in something cashmere with the name Juicy on it? Even better—they were in a size small, a size she worked hard for everyday with the jogging and the Tae Bo, and those Firm tapes with the steps and weights. Those were some evil women on those tapes. But right now those insane "step up, step down, lift your leg to the side and do the samba up and over the two-foot step" tyrants were freaking goddesses because Nikki's ass was fitting right into those Juicy sweats.

When she came back out, Derek had not only taken the food and wine onto the front porch, but he'd lit candles all around and had put her Jack Johnson CD on the stereo.

"Hope you don't mind. This is such a great CD. I always wanted to learn to play the guitar. This guy is really good." He was sitting on the porch in her wicker love seat. The dinner plates were in front of him on a matching table.

"Of course I don't mind. But I have to give you some advice about learning to play the guitar. If your musical talent parallels your juggling ability, then don't do it. Just listen to someone else play."

"Harsh. Very, very harsh."

She laughed and sat down next to him, brushing up against his bare arm. He'd rolled up the sleeves on his button-down shirt after taking off his jacket and tie.

"Soft. Nice," he said. "Your outfit I mean, because *you* are a mean woman."

"Yes, well, it is something I pride myself in. I promise I'll be sweet for the rest of the night, but I can't promise what might happen when the clock strikes midnight." She picked up her wine glass, which he refilled. "You sure know how to treat a girl." She bit her lip the minute the sentence rolled off her tongue. God, how dumb could one sound? She hadn't been a girl for over twenty years.

"Yeah, no kidding, especially after taking you to a wedding where the bride dies and you find her."

Thank God, his comeback was almost as dumb as hers. "It was really weird finding her like that."

"Let's not talk about it."

He raised his glass for a toast. "To you."

"Me? Why?"

"Why not? You've lasted here for half a year, and you deserve a toast after what these past months have thrown your way. After tonight, I figure I better at least toast you, because, if I were you, I'd be running from the wine country as fast as I could."

"I'm not going anywhere. Not much scares me away."

"So we'll drink to you, my unafraid, ever curious um . . ."

"Assistant?"

"No. Friend."

She brought her glass up. "I'll drink to that."

They clinked their crystal together. She couldn't help but follow Derek's lips from the time they touched the glass until he moved it away. And when his eyes caught hers, she could've sworn he'd been watching her in the same way.

"So, what's up with you and Andrés?" he asked, setting his wine glass down.

"What do you mean?" she asked.

"What do I mean? Like you don't know? Come on, Nikki, I've seen the way he looks at you and I've also seen the way he hugs you and always gives you that almost too-nice of a kiss on your cheek, whether it's to say hello or goodbye."

Was someone jealous here? If she didn't know better, she'd think that maybe Derek had been bitten by the green-eyed monster. "We're just friends. That's all. Like you and me."

Derek raised his eyebrows in mock pretense. "If that's what you think, I mean about you and Andrés, then you're blind, because he is *after* you."

"I think you've got it wrong there. How is your love life going, by the way? Tara Beckenroe still chasing you around town at every opportunity?"

"The blonde devil? Yeah, she's a royal pain."

"No kidding. Talk about somebody who has the hots for someone. She's not going to give up until she sinks those phony acrylic claws in you."

"She'll have to do it after I'm dead and six feet under, because Tara Beckenroe is certainly not my type."

Nikki looked pointedly at him. His comment getting her interest. "What is your type?"

Derek leaned back against the sofa. "That's a loaded question. I haven't thought much about it since Meredith," he replied, referring to his ex-wife. "Tell me, is Andrés Fernandez your type?"

"You don't get off that easy. You didn't answer my question. And I don't know if Andrés is my type. I mean, do we really have to have types? Isn't falling in love or liking someone and falling for them more of a natural progression than simply type casting, and searching out that perfect 'type,' or what you think is that perfect type? At my age . . ."

"Oh right, you're so old."

She socked him lightly on the shoulder. "You know what I'm saying. At least for women in their late thirties and on, forming relationships takes a different path than it once did. In your twenties it's all about who is the hot guy, but I'm finding that friendship and a building of trust is what creates a real attraction." What a bunch of crap. The fact was, yeah Derek was a great guy and someone she felt close to because they'd built a friendship, but when it came down to it, he was not a hard man to look at. His baby blues, square jawline and tanned biceps were still the initial attraction.

"I feel the same way, too."

"What a cop-out."

"Goes both ways," Derek replied. "I'll let you off the hook for now."

"Let me off the hook? Ha! You're the one getting away with avoiding answering the third degree about relationships."

"It's all a matter of point of view. I'll change the subject. Let's talk about your family."

Nikki groaned. That was an even more difficult subject. "I've told you, my aunt raised me. I was born in Tennessee, thus the very slight, once in a blue moon accent. My parents were poor. My father was killed in a car accident and my mom sent me to California to live with my aunt."

"I know that's the short version, but I want to know more. I want to know about your childhood, your friends, where you went to school, all of it."

"It's boring." She waved a hand in the air. "It really is."

"Fine, tell me about your teenage years, by then you were in California with your aunt. She must be quite a gal."

"She is. Definitely." Nikki didn't mind talking about Aunt Cara who meant everything to her and was really the only mother she'd ever known.

As she was about to say, "Let's talk about the vineyard," which would be a safe topic, a car's tires squealed off the payment from Highway 29 and sped into the Estate. They could see its headlights coming their way. The next thing they knew a Porsche Carerra pulled up in front of the cottage. Nikki's jaw dropped. She looked over at Derek who crossed his arms in front of him.

Ah, the Boys of Summer. Nikki and Derek watched as Simon—Derek's half brother, and his lover, Marco, stepped out of the car. When Nikki signed on at Malveaux she'd dubbed the two nitwits with her Boys of Summer tag and they in turn had a pet name for her.

"Goldilocks, you're still here," Simon said. "I thought after that bad business with the murders and all last year, you would've taken your pretty tail back on down to the City of Angels. We were hoping to stay in the cottage."

Marco swaggered up to the porch and batted his long eyelashes at them. In his Italian accent he said, "I'm happy you're here, *Bellisima*. You make this place interesting.

And, look, do I detect love in the air?" Marco pointed to the now emptied wine glasses.

"That's not exactly a shockaroonie. We knew it was a matter of time before you two were shacking up. Mommie Dearest must be beside herself."

"We're not 'together,' you morons. We're simply having dinner," Derek replied.

"God, you two are so silly. Why don't you get it over with? Get it on already and we can all go forward with our lives," Simon said.

"Boys, be good and go stay at a B and B in town, please," Derek said.

"And miss the fun? No way. We're going up to the main house. Let's do lunch tomorrow, Goldilocks. We have so much to tell. We've been Zenning out in Sedona and found the most marvelous of gurus. His name is Guru Sansibaba, and I'm telling you, both Marco and I are changed men. Material things mean nothing. We're like the openhearted, open souls to the world and our fellow man and woman, of course, that our spirit guides have so graciously shown us how to become."

"Along with Guru Sansibaba," Marco said.

"Yes, of course," Simon replied.

"That's obvious with the convertible there. What happened to the fashion shows in New York?" Nikki pointed to the Porsche.

"Yes, well, just because we know materialism is a fruitless path, we don't have to deny ourselves in this life," Marco said. "Simon wanted to get rid of the Mercedes. This is a fit for our new image. The shows in New York disappointed me. I don't think I have the need to design for that world any longer."

"Interesting. And as far as the Porsche goes, well, I can totally see how the rest of the world might not think of a

Porsche as a materialistic person's kind of car," Nikki said.

"See you love bugs tomorrow." Simon got behind the wheel and he and Marco tore up the road toward the main house.

"I've really missed them," Nikki said.

"Yeah, right."

"Simon does seem a bit more chipper, he's usually sour-faced and nasty. I thought he was almost nice."

"It won't last. Here, I'll help you clear the plates."

Even though Nikki wasn't especially pleased to see the return of the boys after they'd been gone for several months, she was happy they'd provided the distraction they had. Derek dropped the topics of discussion for the evening. With the dishes washed, he stretched, letting out a yawn.

"Tired?" Nikki asked.

"A bit."

"Yeah, me, too, it's been a long day."

"Tuesday, right? Dinner? I have to go out of town for a couple of days to take care of some charity business, but we are on for Tuesday?"

"Absolutely." The other day Derek had invited her to come to dinner on Tuesday with him and their accountant, to discuss some business. She loved the fact that he was so involved with the Leukemia Foundation. He was very hands-on and had been for years. His mother had passed away from the terrible disease when he was a kid, and he'd kept her memory going by dedicating much of his time to helping find a cure.

"I'll call when I get in." He kissed her on the cheek. His kiss was different than Andrés'. It was sweet and tender. Andrés' kiss always came with a sense of urgency and electrifying energy. Derek's kiss on the cheek was like melting chocolate candies inside the mouth. Yummy.

He left and she went into her room, flopping down on the bed. With a sigh she reflected on the day's and evening's events from the morbid and horrific to the light and funny, and she smiled at the tinge of romance that filled the air. At least she allowed herself to believe it. What was life without some fantasy to string you along?

However, her last thoughts before drifting to sleep weren't pleasant. The first was a memory of the past—something she wanted to forget. When she was seven she'd been in a car accident that had killed the man she'd always thought was her father, only later discovering that they were not related at all. She'd been hurt badly in the accident, spending two weeks in a coma before her mother shipped her off to California to be raised by her Aunt Cara. She didn't want to think about the one thing that she and Susan Jennings Waltman had in common—the lack of a mother. But Nikki didn't care if she ever saw her mother again. The next and final thought she had before sleep overtook her had to do with the photos she'd seen of Susan Jennings, and who it was Susan had been having sex with in those pictures—Blake Sorgensen.

Chile-Rubbed Chicken, Mango, and Avocado Salad with Franciscan Oakville Estate's Cabernet Sauvignon

Let's say it's been a long night and maybe you didn't come across a dead body or have to cut the evening short with the man of your dreams due to unwelcome visitors, but you have your own reasons for wanting to mix up something easy, fun, healthy and fast. Keep in mind that Nikki does like to roast a chicken or two on Sunday afternoons to have on hand during the week. This is great whether you're a single gal, a committed woman, or in charge of a family because you can use chicken for a variety of meals, including sack lunches. If you don't prepare your chicken ahead of time, then it will take you a little more time to throw this dish together and your chicken will be warm. However, the flavors will still be delicious and you can open wine while you're sautéing the chicken breasts in the chile rub. One to try is Franciscan Oakville Estate's Cabernet Sauvignon. This wine has bold earth flavors of coffee, tobacco, and toasted oak, making it a full-bodied, rich wine with a maturity that leaves the oenophile desiring more as the supple tannins provide a lingering finish.

If you like a white wine or a wine that has a bit of a sweeter taste to it, one to try that would complement this dish would be a Riesling. Rieslings are usually a good choice with Thai or Mexican dishes as they work well with warm spices. They also pair well with light and fruity dishes, so this is a perfect match because of the mango and spice. An excellent value and delicious Riesling comes from V. Sattui. You can only order their wines online, but it is well worth it. A blend of Riesling and Muscat, this slightly sweet white is a great party or picnic wine. It matches well with so many foods, it's refreshing to drink and it commands a modest price.

> 3 tbsp brown sugar
> ¼ cup water
> ¼ cup plus 2 tbsp fresh lime juice, plus lime
>   wedges for serving
> 1 tbsp red chile powder
> 1 tsp chipotle chile powder
> 1 clove crushed garlic
> ¼ cup vegetable oil
> Salt and pepper
> One 3 lb roasted chicken, skin removed, meat
>   shredded (3 cups)
> 1 ripe mango, peeled and cut in ½ inch chunks
> 3 scallions thinly sliced
> 5 oz mesclun (6 cups)

Roasting the chicken: Clean and season the chicken with salt, pepper, or poultry seasonings, and ancho chile powder. Place on a rack in a shallow roasting pan and cook at 450° for 15–20 minutes. This will seal the juices. Then reduce the heat to 375°. There is no need to baste the chicken. Length will vary with the size of the chicken. The best method to tell if it's ready is with a meat thermometer placed in the thickest part of the thigh, which should read between 175°–180°. Once the chicken is roasted, allow it time to cool before shredding and preparing the salad.

In a small saucepan, bring the brown sugar and water to boil. Transfer to a large bowl. Whisk in the lime juice chilé powder, chipotle powder, and garlic; let cool. Whisk in the oil and season with salt and pepper. Add the chicken, mango, and scallions and toss thoroughly with the dressing. Add the mesclun and gently toss. Transfer the salad to plates and serve with lime wedges.

If you decide to sauté the chicken breasts, sauté over medium-high heat in sauté pan with a tablespoon of oil. Season chicken with salt and pepper. Brown the chicken on each side. When finished, dice chicken and proceed with recipe as above.

Chapter 6

Nikki called Isabel several times on Sunday, leaving messages on her machine. She was very worried about her friend. Late Sunday night Isabel returned Nikki's call and explained to her that she'd gone for a long hike in Skyline Wilderness Park, needing the fresh air.

"I would've gone with you," Nikki told her.

"I am sorry. I needed to give myself time alone. I wanted to think. Andrés does not understand why I am as saddened as I feel with concern to the wedding and the death of Susan. You have to promise to me, Nikki, that you will not tell my brother that Kristof and I had a relationship."

Nikki bit her lip and sat down at her kitchen table, looking outside her window at the hills of grapevines now beginning to flourish with the first hint of sugared bulbs, soon ready to turn from fruit into wine. "I think you should tell him. He loves you and he's your brother. He's not stupid,

Isabel. I think he'll figure this all out eventually. You two had to have been spotted by someone around town and the rumors will spread."

"I do not feel that way. I told you that Kristof told me stories to keep everything in regard to us quiet. He said that it was important for us to grow our relationship in that way and keep it from the eyes of the town gossips."

Nikki rolled her eyes. "You were a sucker, my friend."

"I do know this."

They chatted for a few more minutes and Nikki finally got off the phone, feeling better about Isabel's mental state. A hike through the wine country air could do wonders for a person.

Nikki woke up Monday morning and found herself swamped in work. The week before she'd gotten behind, what with her daydreaming over what was supposed to be the perfect not-real date on Saturday. Oddly enough, she really didn't have any complaints, except the part about finding Susan's body. That had put a damper on things. With Derek out of the office, she not only had to make her calls for the day, she also had to clear his agenda and follow through with a few extra items he'd laid across her desk. Around four o'clock a handful of bigwigs from San Francisco were scheduled for a visit to the winery. They were considering carrying Malveaux wines in their restaurants. Derek usually liked to deal with the rich and pompous; he had a good way with people and knew how to handle them. Today, however, Nikki had to play the game.

She put together a cheese and appetizer tray to complement the wines she planned on having the group taste.

Of course, they arrived fifteen minutes late and the leader of the group, David-pronounced-"Daveed" Kistler, Nikki immediately mentally dubbed him Kiss Ass. On Daveed's arm was a slinky, blond *Playboy*-looking model, who walked in asking to buy a set of crystal goblets she'd spotted in the gift shop as they came in. Daveed's immediate response, "Of course, baby girl, whatever you want."

"Nice to meet you. I'm Nikki Sands." Daveed took her hand and shook limply like she might break if actually given a real handshake. God, how she hated that.

The model nodded. "I'm Angel. Just Angel."

Daveed let out a stupid sounding laugh. "Isn't she adorable? I love a woman with one name. Angel. Wow—it's so fitting."

Was there a barf bag around anywhere? Nikki went behind the counter provided for private tastings. Angel giggled like a little six-year-old girl. How was Nikki going to get through this tasting without either vomiting or cracking up? There was only one answer. Drink with them, because apparently they had already been having some fun throughout the wine country.

As she started to pour, another man came in. "Sorry I'm late," the man said. "I'm Daveed's partner, Roman Pangilini," he said.

Nikki was soon pleased that Roman had joined the group, because while Daveed was playing showman to his playmate, Roman was the only one really absorbed and interested in Nikki's wine display and tasting.

After several tastes, talk turned to the events over the weekend. "Did you know the bride who died out at the Waltman Castle over the weekend? Someone at one of the other wineries was telling us about it." Roman took a sip of the red wine Nikki was now pouring.

"I'd met her."

"Me, too, briefly, in the city when I was working the deal to buy out the chain."

This sparked Nikki's interest. "Really? How?"

"I was only introduced to her while I met with Antoine Ferrino about buying out his restaurants. He was married to her friend Martha or Megan. God, what was her name? You know, she kind of made it big for awhile in the Victoria's Secret catalogue and then one day you just didn't see her anymore."

"Pamela?"

"That's it. Pamela." Roman snapped his fingers.

"Pamela Leiland was married to Antoine Ferrino?" Nikki hadn't known that tidbit. Antoine Ferrino had started a chain of gourmet Italian restaurants. There were a handful sprinkled across the country in cosmopolitan cities.

"Oh, yeah. Part of the reason he wanted to sell was because they wanted kids and since Antoine wasn't exactly a young guy, he and Pamela wanted to get moving on it. He figured he hadn't been around to see his other kids grow up, because he'd been so busy starting his restaurants, so if Pamela was going to get pregnant, he wanted to have a second chance to do it right. I met her and the bride, Susan, I think it was, over dinner at the restaurant one night."

"That didn't happen. The pregnancy thing," Daveed interrupted. Angel had spread herself out in one of the oversize lounge chairs and was more than two sheets to the wind. "Right after the buyout, the poor guy died of a heart attack. Pamela was devastated. Weird, but I think she really loved him. It was like 'Beauty and the Beast'—but an old beast and a young beauty."

Nikki turned around to grab another bottle of wine to open. And, hmmm? You are considered what, now? She faced back around with a smile on her face. "That's horrible." She was wondering if Daveed didn't realize that he appeared to be in the same class as Antoine Ferrino, or at least almost. Daveed had to be in his midfifties. Angel not over twenty-five. From what Nikki had seen of Pamela, though, she was fairly bright. Nikki knew that Angel couldn't even hold a candle to Ollie the dog in the brains department.

"Pamela made out okay, money wise. There wasn't as much there as anyone thought. We bought him out at a good price, but Antoine was a bit of a gambler and not just with horses and poker. He'd made some bad investments in the stock market and lost. What he had left, his kids and Pamela divided. It was too bad, about a couple a mil is what I heard."

"A couple million, that's it?" Angel sat up.

Even drunk the word *million* meant something to the wannabe starlet. She sounded mortified. Then she laughed. "That would only be enough for a year's worth of shopping. A real woman couldn't live off of that for long."

Daveed joined her laughter and went to her side. Couldn't this sucker see how he was being played? Probably. The sad thing was he more than likely didn't care. The scene was almost pitiful. How empty the two of them had to be. And was it likely that Pamela Leiland wasn't exactly like them? Nikki got the feeling Susan had been like them, only she'd gotten lucky with Kristof—not only was he filthy rich, but young and handsome. Well, she hadn't been that lucky because she wasn't around to reap the rewards.

After Nikki made a huge sell to the May-December couple and their sidekick and said her goodbyes, she headed back to her cottage and drank a tablespoon of Pepto Bismol to ease the nausea they'd caused. But it had been a worthwhile visit, both financially and mentally stimulating.

Just as she sat down on her couch, threw her legs up on the coffee table and picked up the latest Jennifer Crusie novel, the phone rang. She let it go to the answering machine, until she heard Andrés' voice come across.

"Nikki? You there?"

She grabbed the phone. "Hi. What's up? You sound a bit off?"

"It's Isabel. She's been arrested for the murder of Susan Jennings."

Chapter 7

Nikki met Andrés at the sheriff's main office for Sonoma
County, located in Santa Rosa.

McCall greeted them. "She's being booked down at the
jail. I'm afraid that you can't see her until tomorrow morning at the arraignment."

"What about an attorney? If you read her her rights,
didn't she call an attorney? You obviously brought her in for
questioning and for that, she is entitled to have an lawyer
present," Nikki said.

McCall shrugged. "Guess she's going to need one. And,
yes, we offered her one when we asked her to come in for
questioning. However, she refused."

"You asked her to come in, and she came willingly?
Doesn't that say something about her innocence? This is ludicrous. Isabel wouldn't hurt anyone." Nikki could hear the
anger in her voice and tried to shove it down. It wouldn't be
to anyone's benefit to get emotional with the detective. Aunt

Cara had taught her that in retelling many of her case situations over the years. Always keep your cool, especially when dealing with authority.

"Maybe it says something about her guilt," McCall replied.

"What kind of evidence do you have against her?" Andrés asked, his face almost the color purple. Nikki wanted to calm him down, but she knew of his deep love for his sister and figured he had to be boiling over with rage.

"I can't discuss this with you right now. You'll have to speak with her and her attorney."

"She doesn't have an attorney yet." Andrés clenched his fists and raised his voice an octave, between gritted teeth he said, "And you won't let us see her."

McCall crossed his arms in front of him and rocked back and forth on his long legs. He eyed Nikki, who took it as a warning.

She placed a hand on Andrés' arm. "Let me talk with him, okay? Just settle down, go grab a cup of coffee. No, water, definitely water." Right now, caffeine wouldn't be a good option for her friend.

"Settle down? *Ay, este idiota no mandeja a mi hermana. Pendejo.*" He pointed at McCall.

Nikki understood enough Spanish to know what Andrés had said, and by the looks of McCall he caught the gist as well. It was far from a compliment.

"Trust me, go and get some water."

Andrés stormed off.

Nikki sighed heavily, and looked back up at the detective. "He's understandably upset. I'm sorry. Think about his position for a moment. There's no way Isabel could've murdered Susan. It's impossible. What evidence could you have against her? Can't you please tell me, so we know what we're dealing with and can talk with an attorney. Please?"

"We have protocols, Miss Sands. There are visiting hours at the jail and they are fairly stringent. In the morning she'll be provided with a public defender who will meet with her, and then I assume she can meet with you. That is, unless Mr. Fernandez or Miss Fernandez herself hires a defense attorney on their own."

She took a step closer toward McCall, and against her better judgment put on her bad-acting hat. She touched his arm and smiled. "I realize it's not normal procedure, but you have to understand Isabel isn't from around here, she's not even from this country. You saw her. Does she really look capable of murder?"

McCall shook his head. "She may be a pretty woman, but that doesn't mean she didn't kill Susan Jennings. Trust me, I've arrested other beautiful women before."

"Right. Well, can't you give me some indication as to what she's facing?"

He sighed. "Here's the deal. Mrs. Waltman was poisoned. The autopsy showed that she had enough of a poison called Sodium Fluoroacetate in her system to shut it down within minutes."

"How do you think she got it into her system? If it's a poison, are you thinking food, drink, what? If that's where you're headed, you know as well as I do that Isabel Fernandez was not the only one preparing the meals that night. For that matter, there were a ton of people who had contact with Susan that night." If this was what they were basing Isabel's arrest on, Nikki already knew there was no way it would ever stand up in a court of law.

"We received a call this morning from the trucking company that Isabel Fernandez contracted for the Waltman wedding. Seems they were cleaning out the trucks and they found a vial of some white powder. The climate around the world being what it is, the man I spoke with, didn't know what he'd discovered and thought it might be cocaine, but admitted it could be something else. We ran it through the lab and discovered that it was the poison that matched with Mrs. Waltman's toxicology report."

"How can you pin that on Isabel? There were several drivers and workers using the trucks that day."

"The vial fell out of a sweater that was in the truck. The sweater was part of a uniform and across the chest was Isabel's name."

This was not good at all, but still possibly circumstantial. Wasn't it?

"I can't say any more." McCall nodded his head toward the desk clerk.

Nikki got the picture. "Thanks. But can I ask you one more favor? Can we at least say hello to her and let her know that we're here for her?"

McCall frowned and shook his head. He paused for a moment, looking at her, arms crossed in front of him. Nikki put on her "poor, pitiful me" face.

"I'll see what I can do. Maybe I can pull some strings over at the main detention facility. However . . ." He held up his hand. "You need to explain to Mr. Fernandez to pipe down. I know exactly what *pendejo* means."

An hour later, McCall's string pulling had worked and they were facing Isabel at an interview table inside the jail. She was in handcuffs, her face tear-stained with black mascara running down it. Nikki gasped at the sight of her and her throat constricted to keep from crying out. She wanted to hug her, but McCall had instructed there'd be no touching. Andrés' face grew taut and his eyes welled with tears at the sight of his sister, an anguished, stricken look accompanying the orange jumpsuit she'd been made to wear.

In Spanish, Andrés told his sister how much he loved her and not to worry.

"I did not kill her," Isabel said. She placed her face in her palms and wept.

"Of course you didn't. We're going to get you out of here," Nikki replied. She wanted to be strong for her friend, but it was difficult, especially seeing her like this. Broken down and lost. Nikki recognized the signs and knew that Isabel was suffering from shock.

"I promise to you both, that I would not do this deed they accuse me of." She slumped back in the chair she was in, tears continuing to stream down her face.

"I have an attorney coming to see you in the morning. He couldn't get over here tonight, but he'll be by early before the arraignment. I was told he's the best defense attorney in this county. It's going to be okay," Andrés said.

Nikki could tell that Andrés was trying hard to remain strong for his sister, as she wanted to. He was doing a much better job than she was, however, and Nikki knew that it couldn't be easy.

After a few more minutes of trying to console Isabel, McCall told them they had to go.

Once inside the car, Andrés fumed, swearing about the injustice and how wrong it all was. "What could they have on her? Why arrest my sister? She wouldn't kill Susan Jennings."

"No, she wouldn't. I spoke with the detective and he gave me some info about why they arrested her." Nikki went on to explain to Andrés what McCall had told her back at the station. Her information only infuriated Andrés even further and he began swearing again in his native tongue.

Nikki touched his arm. "You have to calm down and be rational for Isabel. It's dinnertime. I know a great place close by where we can get a bite to eat and we can maybe come up with something, at least a strategy for Isabel."

"I don't think I could eat. I'm too upset."

"I'm with you, but if we take some time to try and relax a minute, you might be able to get yourself together and concentrate on the problem here, instead of getting yourself all worked up. That won't solve anything, and it certainly won't get Isabel out of jail. We can't do anything tonight about this, other than talk and think."

He nodded, took a deep breath, and took her directions to Capri Ristorante in downtown Santa Rosa. The restaurant was an Italian place with an eclectic setting, both rustic and contemporary, done in brick, chrome and cobalt blues, with high ceilings that sported skylights. It was definitely Nikki's favorite when she got over into Santa Rosa on occasion, not only for the atmosphere and delicious fare, but also for the owner, Luigi—a charismatic, old-school Italian with all the airs of a romantic. As they entered the restaurant, Luigi greeted them, kissing Nikki on both cheeks.

"I've missed you, Bella. Why you no come by before now?" He took both of her hands in his and held them out openly.

"I'm sorry. Life gets crazy."

"Never too crazy for a good food and a little of romance." He winked at her and turned to Andrés. "This is your boyfriend, no?"

She shook her head.

Luigi took Andrés hand and pumped it. "He should be. He's a fine, strong man. You two take a table by the window. I will be over in a moment, and bring you a vino that is special to me."

Andrés tried to be more cheerful, but as he sat in the seat across from her in the restaurant, he could only stare out the window. She let him wind down before again bringing up Isabel's situation.

It was over dishes of veal with artichokes in a marsala sauce for Nikki, the pork tenderloin for Andrés, and a bottle of zinfandel, that Nikki and Andrés hashed out Isabel's predicament and Nikki was able to file away some interesting information that Andrés had.

"Wait a minute, you actually overheard Susan and Kristof arguing the other day?"

"More than an argument. Those two were like a horse and a snake. It was out in the parking lot at Grapes when they'd come by to sign off on the contract with Isabel."

"Do you know what they were saying?"

"He was pretty much telling her that she was being unreasonable and that he didn't like that side of her."

"Hmmm." Nikki took a sip of her wine. "What else?"

"She yelled at him to not marry her if he felt she was being unreasonable. I thought he should have backed out when she said that. I would have. He told her that maybe he wouldn't marry her. Then she started to cry after that and he hugged her. They made up."

"What if they did, but didn't?" Nikki asked.

"I don't understand."

"Maybe Kristof was starting to see the real Susan in all of her phony glory."

"You think he could've killed her?"

Nikki shrugged. "Maybe him, or someone who loves him. Like his dad, or another woman, even his aunt Sara."

"Why not do the right thing and not marry her? Why go to the extreme? Not only did he have to commit murder, but then he also would have had to frame my sister."

"Someone did frame your sister. We know that."

Andrés looked out the window again. "Yes."

"It's a good question, why not just end the upcoming nuptials and be done with her? Here's a thought. The Waltmans are very rich people, from their wines to the land they've developed in the county and on and on. Rich people, well, all people really, usually have some well kept, hidden secrets. What if the Waltmans have some juicy tidbit lying around in their closet, and Susan stumbled onto that skeleton? You can't tell me that Kristof hadn't seen the ugly side of his future wife before the day you saw them arguing."

"It's hard to imagine. What kind of secret do you think they could have?"

"No clue, but if Susan knew what that secret was and was blackmailing Kristof, the killer could've murdered Susan to protect Kristof."

"The future bride blackmailing the groom?" Andrés asked.

"There is quite a bit to be gained for whoever does finally wind up with Kristof Waltman. If there was no prenup, and down the line Susan decides it's time to cut ties and take that community property with her, well, I guarantee she would've made out better than if she'd agreed to a cash payoff from the get go. Plus, she'd have the Waltman name for the rest of her life to get her through closed doors."

"It's a theory, I suppose."

"Yes, it is, and maybe a feasible one. People have been known to kill over secrets. And if there is one the Waltmans have been keeping, then I intend to discover it."

Pork Tenderloin
with Port Wine Mushroom Sauce
with Alexander Valley
Vineyards Sin Zin

This pork tenderloin dish is delicious and easy to prepare, although it tastes so good that your significant other will likely think you spent your day in the kitchen. When ready to serve, open a bottle of Sin Zin from Alexander Valley Vineyards. This is a great wine to drink with this earthy dish as it contains mature fruit flavors of strawberry, plum, and cherry blended with coffee beans, black pepper, and peppermint.

> 1 lb pork tenderloin
> 1 lb cleaned, thinly sliced cremini or button
>   mushrooms
> Fresh ground black pepper and salt to taste
> 1 clove garlic crushed
> 2 tbsp olive oil
> ½ stick butter
> ½ cup of rich dessert Port wine

Over medium-high heat, heat olive oil in heavy skillet, preferably cast-iron. While skillet heats, make paste of black pepper, salt, and garlic, and rub this mixture into the tenderloin on all sides. Cook 2–3 minutes per side. Remove pork to platter and keep warm.

Add butter to the skillet, scraping up the good seasonings as the butter melts. Add the mushrooms and cook over medium heat until they begin to render their moisture. Add the port wine and place pork loin back in mixture and allow sauce to reduce by half. If you wish, you may add 1 tablespoon of flour to thicken the sauce.

Remove pork loin, slice into thin slices, and pour sauce evenly. A good side is grilled asparagus and mashed sweet potatoes. Bon Appetit!

Chapter 8

The next morning was as horrible as the events from the day before. Isabel's arraignment, regardless of the wonderful defense attorney Andrés hired, turned out dismally. The judge would not release her on bail, citing that she was a flight risk because she had been in the United States for just under two years, and he felt that she might possibly flee to Spain. Andrés stayed behind after the arraignment to see Isabel, but Nikki had to get to work. She also wanted to see what she could find out about a possible prenuptial agreement between Susan and Kristof.

Instead of taking the freeway back into Napa, Nikki had the compulsion to go the long way through Sonoma and to pass by the Waltman Castle. She'd just have to add on some extra time at work that afternoon.

Passing by the castle, she continued to wonder if some dark secret resided within those walls. She thought about stopping and seeing who might be around, but on what pretense? She was sure that if there were any lurking detectives or crime scene specialists hanging out, they wouldn't appreciate her interrupting their job. However, she still believed the theory that she and Andrés had conjured up the night before might prove a valid one, and knew that she would have to make a surprise visit in the next day or two. With that thought, she decided to go into Sonoma Square to pick up a sympathy card for Kristof, et al., and use it as her excuse to drop in. A flimsy one, yes, but still an excuse. She'd take the card over after work.

How plans had changed by the time she left Sonoma Square . . .

She stepped outside the local card and gift shop, and stopped in her tracks. Seated across the street at the Ledson Hotel & Restaurant at one of the outside tables—granted it was a corner table and somewhat blocked by a post—having what looked to be a cozy lunch together was none other than Kristof Waltman and Deirdre Dupree. Kristof had some gall, now didn't he? Wasn't he supposed to be the bereaved widower? Odd to be out and about with none other than your former girlfriend.

She wished she had a damn camera because if she had, Detective McCall's focus might take a different direction.

They were partaking in early afternoon liquid vine. Not only was Deirdre Dupree Kristof's previous love, she was also the corporate sales manager at Waltman Castle. Nikki had heard their breakup had been nasty, but that Marty Waltman loved Deirdre, who did a phenomenal job for him. And, with some bonuses and a major pay raise, she'd stayed on. Rumor had it that Deirdre was the one who initiated the breakup after a wild weekend out in the city where she'd hooked up with an old flame.

Funny thing was that at that moment neither Kristof

nor Deirdre looked too unhappy to be in each other's company. Nikki walked into the Church Mouse Thrift Shop and continued to watch from behind the front window while feigning interest in a pair of candleholders. The two looked to be talking animatedly, and from what Nikki could see from her vantage point, with even a laugh or two here and there.

Then, a real poignant moment when Deirdre leaned across the table and wiped what Nikki presumed was a tear from Kristof's face. Okay, maybe he was really in mourning and she was being a pal and getting him out of the house. Hard to swallow, but maybe. Could their lunch simply be an old friend comforting another? Or, could it mean something more? Nikki had to find out.

She went back to her car and looked up Deirdre's cell phone number in her Day-Timer. They'd met at a wine-making event about a month earlier and found they had some things in common. Since then, Nikki had met Deirdre a couple of times for coffee, so calling her might not seem totally out of the blue. Then again, it might, but she had to do it.

Deirdre picked up after a few rings. "Hey, Deirdre. It's me, Nikki Sands, over at Malveaux."

"Oh, hello."

Was that a bit of strain Nikki heard in the other woman's voice? "Listen, I've been talking to Derek about doing some diversifying with his wine and he's considering buying some of the grapes over there in your neck of the woods. I tasted some of your wines while at the wedding the other night and don't say anything to my boss, but I really found your pinot superior to the pinots we're making." Nikki had learned that a bit of lying was required while snooping into the lives of others. She didn't consider it lying exactly, because it was really a means to an end, and wasn't the end about getting to the truth? "I know I should probably be calling Marty or Kristof, but it's such a difficult time for them, I'm sure. Plus, I want your opinion and ideas about how I should talk to Derek about it. And we keep talking about getting together. Why don't we have dinner tonight? My treat."

"Um, yeah, okay."

"Great. I'll meet you at the square at six."

Nikki hung up the phone with a sense of purpose and started the car. Halfway back to Napa, her cell phone rang. "Hello."

"Nikki, it's me Derek. I'm in Houston right now, getting ready to board my plane. We still on for tonight?"

Crap! How could she have forgotten her dinner with Mr. Luscious? In all the hubbub with Isabel's arrest and disappointing arraignment, and then seeing Kristof with Deirdre she'd lost it and forgotten her dinner plans for the evening. Nikki coughed and first thought maybe she should tell him that she didn't feel good. No. Lying to Derek wasn't an option.

"Derek, I'm so sorry, but I can't. Something else has come up that can't wait. I hope you understand. Can we do it later this week? Mr. Lareby can join us," she said, referring to the accountant who was supposed to have been meeting with them over dinner. "How about Friday? Can we do dinner at my place?"

He didn't answer for a few seconds and she figured she'd totally blown any chance she might ever have had with him.

But then he finally said, "Friday sounds good. Better actually, because it'll be the weekend and we can wind down. We can meet with Mr. Lareby another time. We won't have to worry about getting up early for work, so we can make it casual. I'll bring a movie with me. Sound good?"

"Yeah. It sounds great." They agreed on a time and Nikki flipped shut her phone and then let out a yelp of glee. Dinner at her house on a Friday night, and a movie to boot. Now that *sounded* like a date.

Chapter 9

Nikki arrived at the Sonoma Plaza a tad early. She wanted to request a table off in the corner somewhere, hoping that she could get Deirdre to loosen her lips about the comings and goings at the Waltman Castle. She didn't want her to be shy for fear of prying ears. They'd decided to meet at Della Santina's, a little trattoria-type place boasting Tuscan flavor, replete with candlelight and romantic Italian music playing in the background. Too bad the dinner had to be with Deirdre.

The hostess seated Nikki out on the brick-covered patio surrounded by flowers that popped with brilliant color next to the black and white decor of the tables and linens. A waiter placed a basket of fresh crusty bread in front of her. She checked her watch and regretted that she was supposed to be at that very moment sitting across from Derek at Hurley's Restaurant in Yountville. Not that she didn't love Della Santina's. It truly was a wonderful place, but it was the company she wasn't totally looking forward to. Nikki liked Deirdre fine. She was a nice woman and okay company in a pinch. But Deirdre Dupree certainly wasn't Derek Malveaux.

However, this dinner could prove to be important, and maybe somehow, during conversation, something would slip from Deirdre's mouth that could lead to Susan's killer. Once again, Nikki found herself caught up in a mystery where she knew she shouldn't be, but she really couldn't help herself. She actually found some weird pleasure in solving murder mysteries. She figured it had to do with the fact that Aunt Cara had been a homicide detective for the LAPD during the years she'd raised Nikki. During those years Nikki had gone over every police procedural book her aunt stored in the bookshelves in their apartment off of La Brea, fascinated by their contents.

It could also be that although Nikki's short-lived cop show series, which she'd done back in L.A., had bombed badly, she'd liked the idea of being a detective, even if only an imaginary one. Acting hadn't paid off like she'd hoped it would, but it had lent itself in helping her figure out the winemaker's murder. Maybe it would do the same in guiding her to Susan's real killer.

Deirdre Dupree walked into Della Santina's looking her almost too *Sex and the City* self, decked out in a plunging neckline pant suit; all black from head to toe. But she still captured enough girl-next-door that she didn't look sleazy. With a clear complexion, bright blue eyes, her hair worn in the latest Jennifer Aniston style, a dash of freckles across her nose, and a Kate Spade purse hanging from her shoulders, Deirdre Dupree had apparently learned her fashion sense from *In Style Magazine*. And she had gotten pretty good at it. At thirty-three, Deirdre didn't look a day over twenty-five. And that outfit—pretty amazing. Sonoma was a casual, quaint town that didn't sport any women wearing designer duds unless it involved the latest charity event, and so it was sort of odd that she was decked out. Did Deirdre have after dinner plans? Maybe. With her former beau?

"Hey, sorry I'm late," she said as she sat down across from Nikki.

"You're not. I was a bit early."

"I had a hellishly long day, I need a glass of wine. Should I make it a bottle?"

"Why not?" Nikki reflected on her day and wondered how it measured up in comparison to her dinner companion's.

They decided on a bottle of an Italian style wine, but one produced in Sonoma. Nikki decided to get the formalities over with and wait for the wine to be poured. Wine usually loosened lips, and for where Nikki wanted to direct this conversation, she'd need to have Miss Dupree somewhat relaxed. She brought up her phony story about wanting to buy grapes from the Waltman Vineyard.

"We all know that the pinot grapes grow better over here because you're closer to the coast and the grapes like the somewhat cooler climate."

"I have to agree. We grow some spectacular pinot grapes on the Waltman land. I'm partial, though. You know how us Sonomans feel about our grapes versus you Napalites."

They both laughed at the comment as the waiter opened the bottle of Nebbiolo and Nikki nodded her head towards Deirdre to allow her to take the taste test. It held true that the wine country communities had differing opinions about each other's wines, and that each one thought they lived and grew their vines in the better part of the region. They all enjoyed taunting each other in a sarcastic manner over their differences.

They talked a few more minutes about the possibilities of either a straight purchase of pinot grapes from Malveaux or the possibility of doing an exchange.

"I think we have some excellent chardonnay grapes you would find could do wonders for the white wines you're offering."

"It's a thought. I'll run it by Marty when everything settles down at the castle."

Perfect timing to bring it all up, except the waiter showed up at that very moment to take their dinner orders. Nikki settled on the cannelloni. Not too low on the no-carb plan, but damn tasty. Deirdre went the less caloric route and had the roasted turkey breast. Both dishes went well with what they were drinking and since both women were already on their second glass, Deirdre took it upon herself to order another bottle. Nikki didn't protest, but knew in the back of her mind that she'd have to start thinking about alternatives for getting home that evening.

"I take it things are pretty rough around the castle? I can't even imagine," Nikki said.

"You're right about that. Marty is beside himself and trying to comfort the ex-beauty queen."

"Pamela? I thought she was a model."

"Yeah, whatever. You'd think he'd be doing his best to make sure Kristof is all right, but he's been doting on the doe-eyed brunette all this time. She's pretty broken up. I mean she was Susan's best friend. But what about Kristof? Doesn't he count, since he was the woman's new husband?"

"I'm sure you've been a good friend to Kristof, though?"

"I'm trying, but it's so hard. He's really down."

"It must be difficult, considering the two of you were once together." Nikki picked up her glass of wine and swirled the contents in the glass, noticing the legs of the wine that dribbled down the crystal. It was something she loved about wine and she'd learned that the thicker the legs, for the most part, the fuller bodied the wine. If the legs, or tears as the French say, are thin, then the wine is usually light bodied.

"Part of the reason my day was so hellish was I spent it listening to Kristof grieve and carry on about Susan. I'm not heartless. The woman *is* dead." Deirdre finished another glass of wine as the waiter promptly appeared with the second bottle and dinner plates. After he'd served the food and poured the wine, Deirdre glanced around the room, as if to see if anyone was listening. "I hate to say this, but I really feel this way." She lowered her voice to a near whisper. "I'm sad for Kristof because he's obviously hurting, but that woman was bad news, and trust me, he's better off without her. You know what? I'm just glad it was Isabel Fernandez who offed Susan and not me, because trust me, it did cross my mind a time or two. Poor Isabel must've snapped. I saw the news this afternoon saying that she can't even post bail. Too bad, because she seemed like a nice woman, but, God, you never know about people and what might make them do things, like commit murder. She must have some real problems."

Uh, uh, uh. Woman was cruising for a bitch slap. It disgusted Nikki to hear Deirdre talk about Isabel as if she were a nutcase, but knew keeping it together would benefit Isabel far more than winding up in a cell next to her. Deirdre was obviously unaware of the close friendship she had with Isabel, which wasn't a surprise, for as far as Nikki was concerned Deirdre wasn't much more than an acquaintance. All the same, Nikki took a bite of her dinner to prevent herself from mouthing off, and hoped that Deirdre would continue with her diatribe. Thankfully, she did.

"That wedding that took place really should've been his and mine, you know. But Susan Jennings got her hooks into Kristof and we were all over with."

Nikki swallowed hard, and nearly choked on her cannelloni. "Susan was the reason you broke up with Kristof?"

"Oh, you've apparently heard the watered-down version of the story. Well, girlfriend, I'm going to tell you exactly how it goes. First off, I didn't break up with Kristof. He broke up with me. I know the gossip that's traveled. Some ridiculous story about how I went to the city one night and had a kick-ass time with some guy I met at a club and then I came back from my weekend romp—where I was visiting friends—and broke it off with the love of my life. Who, they say, turned around and conveniently found Susan Jennings waiting in the wings to rescue him from his broken heart."

"That was sort of what I heard. I also heard you wanted to leave the winery after the breakup."

"Right. Figures. It was that version of the story that got me so wound up in the first place that I almost left Waltman." Deirdre sipped her wine and then ate a few bites of her dinner before continuing. "The real deal goes like this. I went into the city to hang with some old friends that I'd gone to high school with. My old boyfriend, Hugh, showed up. We got to talking. He made a move, and I shot him down. I came back to the vineyard the next day and I told Kristof everything. He turned it around on me and said that maybe we should have some space to see other people, since I still obviously had open opportunities surrounding me."

"Harsh."

"I know, because that wasn't the case at all. The next thing I know Susan is parading around the castle on the weekends and at every event with Kristof. Then she started bringing Pamela around for Marty. I can't help feeling like it was all contrived. Kristof and I dated for over a year and within two weeks of ending our relationship, he had that woman staying at the castle with him."

"Do you think they were carrying on before you two broke up and he used your visit to the city against you, just so he wouldn't look like the bad guy when he did bring Susan around?" Or, maybe, the blackmail idea *was* a real possibility, thus the pressure to dump Deirdre like a hot potato. But if Susan was blackmailing Kristof, why take a chance and hang out with Isabel on the side?

"Think? I don't have to think it. I know it. Susan basically insinuated it and plenty more to me over the past several months. Wouldn't have put up with her crap, if the money and perks Marty offered me hadn't been so good, because that woman was downright abusive to me."

Nikki felt the wine going to her head and she could tell by Deirdre's slight slur and open-book attitude that it was doing the same to her. There was no love lost between Deirdre and Susan. That much was for sure.

"What else did she do or say to you?" Nikki asked.

"Well, I may have started it one day. I'd tasted some wine with a customer and hadn't spit. Then she came sauntering in when I was finished."

"Uh oh."

"Exactly. I told her she was all wrong for Kristof. Kristof is a softy deep down and I know he wants a family soon. Growing up without his mom left some emptiness there and we used to talk about kids and how much joy they can bring. Something about Susan, I don't know maybe her haute couture clothing, or her continual need to drop a grand a week at the spa doesn't strike me as someone who'd make a great mother. I told her that."

"You didn't."

"I did."

"What did she say to that?" The gossip was getting juicer with each glass of wine.

"Plenty. She actually told me not to worry about the little Waltmans who would be running around the castle in the near future, because that's what nannies were for, and since I seemed so concerned about it, that if I was lucky she'd consider me for the position after she and Kristof were pregnant, because she had no desire to raise and be occupied with children. She added her opinion on kids, saying they were as much a pain in the ass as I was, and that it would be a fitting position for me around the castle."

"She said that?"

"Yep. Exact words."

"You're sure nice to be helping Kristof through this time after all Susan put you through."

"What can I do? I love him. Still. I can't help myself." Tears sprang to Deirdre's eyes. "Will you excuse me?" Deirdre went to the restroom, while Nikki found herself picking up the tab. Yikes. Not cheap with those two bottles of wine thrown in. Sleuthing was an expensive hobby.

With Deirdre in the restroom she had a chance to think about the hatred and jealousy between the two women at the Waltman Castle. It was hard to believe that Deirdre Dupree could possibly be a murderer. However, Deirdre's resentment toward Susan was as obvious as the headache Nikki was sure to wake up with in the morning after all the wine they'd drunk.

There was a lot to get straight about Susan's murder. Impossible at that moment. Gossip and alcohol were swimming in her brain. What Nikki could get straight was that Deirdre would need a cab ride home, and she couldn't drive herself back over the pass to the Malveaux Estate. She'd have to bite the bullet and pay an exorbitant amount in cab fare to get back to Napa. How stupid to have drunk so much wine. She knew better than that, and it kind of worried her that she'd been so reckless and irresponsible. She'd gotten carried away with Deirdre and her story and she'd have to make a note to herself not to allow that to happen again.

Her cell phone rang in the middle of mentally beating herself up, and the question was answered as to how she'd get home when the voice on the other end heard her predicament.

"I'll come and get you. See you in about half an hour."

Cannelloni Florentine
with Pezzi King Vineyard's
Old Vine Zinfandel

Snooping and gossiping are the two hobbies in a woman's life that require carbs. No—seriously. Look at Nikki's situation. She has to solve a murder and dish the dirt with a gal who might actually be the killer! Now, granted, you may never find yourself in this exact situation. However, there has to have been at least a time or two when you found yourself with piqued curiosity where you just had to find out the truth. When that happens, there is no better remedy than energy food, and no matter what, the carbs might slow you down for the night, but the next day . . . you'll be a mad woman, and ready to take on the world. So, go ahead and make a dish that will help you dish the dirt—cannelloni stuffed with spinach and covered in a meat and tomato sauce, which pairs beautifully with Pezzi King Vineyard's Old Vine Zinfandel. This is a big, traditional Zinfandel with strong berry flavors, allspice, and a lingering maple syrup finish. It's a classic!

This recipe does not come straight from Della Santina's, but is user friendly and tastes almost as good.

1 (8 oz) package cannelloni pasta
8 oz ground veal
2 carrots chopped
½ celery stalk, chopped
½ yellow onion, chopped
10 oz spinach, rinsed and chopped

1¼ tsp salt
1¼ tsp pepper
2 tbsp olive oil
2 cups dry white wine
1 cup heavy cream
1 cup Roma (plum) tomatoes, diced
½ cup grated Parmesan cheese
2 tsp Italian seasoning
2 tbsp chopped basil
2 tsp extra virgin olive oil
2 cloves garlic, minced
1 chopped onion
1 tsp salt
1 tsp black pepper
4 leaves fresh basil, chopped

Bring a large pot of lightly salted water to a boil. Add pasta and cook for 8–10 minutes or until al dente; drain, separate shells, and set aside.

Preheat oven to 500°. In a 9×13 baking dish, combine veal, carrots, celery, chopped onion and spinach. Stir well. Stir in 1¼ tsp salt and 1¼ tsp pepper, 2 tbsp olive oil, and white wine. Place in oven and roast until veal is brown and vegetables are soft, 30 to 40 minutes. Stir frequently. If meat begins to smoke, reduce heat to 400°.

Let meat mixture cool 15 minutes, then process in food processor until finely chopped. Return to pan and stir in cream, Roma tomatoes, Parmesan cheese, Italian seasoning, and 2 tbsp basil. Bake 20 minutes more. Remove from oven and let cool.

While meat mixture is cooling enough to handle, make tomato sauce. Puree canned tomatoes with their juice in food processor until smooth. In large skillet over medium heat, heat 2 tbsp virgin olive oil. Sauté garlic and chopped onion until soft. Stir in puréed tomato, 1 tsp salt and 1 tsp pepper. Cook 5–10 minutes, or until no longer watery. Add four chopped basil leaves and cook one more minute.

Reduce oven to 350°. Stuff pasta shells with cooled meat mixture, 2–3 tbsp per shell. Place shells in clean 9 × 13 baking dish. Pour tomato sauce over shells and bake 20 minutes, or until sauce is bubbly.

Chapter 10

After she'd returned from the restroom, Deirdre's senses appeared to have taken hold of her as she'd asked Nikki not to repeat anything that she'd said. She'd also added that she was truly sorry *poor* Susan had been murdered. She didn't buy that Deirdre was totally sorry, but for now Nikki was only accumulating information.

Their conversation turned light as they talked about clothes and movie stars. Nikki never let on to Deirdre that it had once been her dream to be in the spotlight in Hollywood.

Andrés arrived as the women were chatting about Brad Pitt's abs. "Looks like you two are having a grand time," he said. Then he offered to take them home.

The quick ride down the road to Deirdre's house was quiet, as the alcohol seemed to kind of settle in on both women.

Nikki expected a lecture from Andrés once Deirdre was locked safely inside her place, but she was wrong.

"I think it's good that you're making friends and having fun. I wish Isabel was more willing to venture out and meet people." He stopped almost in mid-sentence. "Now, I only hope that she'll have that chance."

"She will. We have to believe that, and I think I could be getting closer to finding out who really killed Susan Jennings."

He looked sharply at her. "What are you talking about, Nikki?"

"You know, I wasn't having a leisurely dinner with Deirdre. I think that would be kind of cold to be out with a 'friend,' while my dear friend sits behind bars. I know how it might have looked to you, but it's not what you think."

"You were fishing, weren't you?"

"Yep, and I think I've set out some bait and we might be able to hook a big fish."

"No, Nikki. I don't like this at all. I know you only want to help Isabel, but the fact is there is a killer out there, and your hunting around like this doesn't sit well with me. I don't want you to get hurt."

"I'm not going to get hurt, and face it, the cops aren't looking any further than your sister. I'll be careful."

"I've got the attorney pushing for more of an investigation from the Sheriff's department. I think that's a better route than putting you in danger."

"Okay, I'll leave it alone and let the police handle it." Means to an end—the truth.

"Nikki . . ." He looked sideways at her.

"I'll be careful, and I'll be discreet. Let me just ask my questions and see what I can find out."

He groaned. "You can be aggravating."

"I've been told that before."

"By your aunt no doubt."

Nikki nodded.

"Isabel is the only family that I have left. I want to be around her. I want her to marry and have kids so I can be an uncle and be a part of a larger family. I'm going to do everything I can to get her out of this mess."

"I agree, and that's what I'm doing."

"Promise me you'll be careful. I'd like to see you have a family too, one day."

"Cross my heart. What about you? Don't you want to marry and have children?"

Andrés shifted the car into lower gear as they started down Oakville Grade. He grew silent for a moment, and in a softer voice replied, "I want to get married and have children more than I can express."

At first Nikki didn't know how to respond. "You just have to find the right woman."

"Who says that I haven't?"

Okay, now Nikki really didn't know how to respond. Ask who? Ignore it? What? What to say? She was happy in that second that she was liquored up. She could use it as an excuse if it ever came up again that she didn't have any recollection of him ever mentioning marriage or the right woman.

They were quiet for several minutes as Andrés wheeled his truck down the hill and into Napa. He turned on the radio. An old Tears For Fears song was playing. "Head Over Heels." When the song got to the chorus, Andrés stole another glance at Nikki. This time there was no meaning lost on her as the singer belted out the words, "Don't break my heart, don't throw it away."

They turned into Malveaux Estate and pulled up next to the cottage. "Why don't you come in for some chai tea?" she asked. In spite of his last comment and the silence between them that had ensued, she didn't want to end the night on that strange note, especially since he'd been so gracious as to take his time to drive to Sonoma and get her tipsy ass home.

"Sounds good."

He turned off the engine and they walked toward the cottage. Reaching the porch, headlights turned down the road and looked to be coming their way, but then they swerved and headed back up the hill.

"What was that all about?" Andrés asked.

"If I had to guess, I'd say that was the Boys of Summer."

"Simon and Marco have graced you with their presence again?"

"You said it. It's always a pleasure to have them around."

After making the tea, they sat and talked late into the evening. She sobered up after a while and enjoyed his company. He was easy to talk to and a good listener, and when he got on the topic of winemaking, the passion in him that she'd noticed when they first met shone through.

"You know that saying about wine and women, how they get better with age? It's true. The comparison, whoever made it, is brilliant," he said.

"Okay, you're gonna have to explain this one to me."

"A young wine is tart and untamed. You never know how the wine is going to taste, like a girl who has entered that stage of being a woman. She's unpredictable, emotional, and unstable. A wine that has sat in the barrel and mellowed is smooth, elegant, sweet with enough tang to be interesting."

"Tell me, what age of woman are you talking about? One who as you say, has all of those refined qualities?"

"I don't think a woman gets truly interesting until she hits at least thirty. Before that, I've discovered that finding the substance is usually difficult. And then, with each year after her third decade, a woman only gets better. My mother in her seventies was one of the most beautiful, interesting and wise women that I've ever known."

Nikki set her teacup down on the coffee table in front of her. "I think you're an exception because lately I've encountered the opposite." She told him about Daveed, and his bunny. She also reflected on Marty and Pamela, but didn't want to bring up the subject of the Waltmans and the wedding gone awry again.

"That's an empty life. It's not for me." He checked his watch. "I've got to get going. I'm going to visit Isabel in the morning and we have another meeting with the attorney." He kissed her cheek, lingering a bit longer than usual.

After he left, Nikki touched the side of her face where his lips had been. She couldn't help wondering what type of life Andrés Fernandez was looking for, and with whom did he want to live it?

Chapter 11

Nikki signed the sympathy card she'd bought the day before and after work took off for the Waltman Castle. She'd thought to add a bouquet of fresh flowers to go along with the card and had made a stop at a florist's.

Sara Waltman opened the door to the castle, and ushered Nikki inside. "Those are beautiful. I'm sure Kristof will appreciate them. But you shouldn't have spent so much. They must have cost a fortune. That gold digger wouldn't have appreciated them. Come on inside and make yourself comfortable in the sitting room. Marty has set out the evening tray of treats and has gone to visit the cellar for some wine. I'm going to change out of my house coat and into something a bit nicer."

Nikki looked down at her khakis and powder blue J. Crew sweater and wondered if the Waltmans dressed for dinner. They didn't seem *that* uptight.

As if Sara had read her mind she said, "I've worn this

all day, and damn if I haven't started to smell like an old woman."

Nikki stifled her laughter at this and reached across to the marble coffee table for a piece of Havarti cheese on Waterman cracked pepper crackers.

She took a glance around the room, and though she'd been inside the castle the other day, she hadn't taken in this room spruced up with chintz, velvet, silks, and damask in shades of cream and pale yellow. The furniture was comfortable but looked way too nice to allow anyone to sit on it. It was twice the size of her cottage and reminded her of the movies she'd seen with an eighteenth-century backdrop where everyone goes to the party and dances around in their flowing gowns with men wearing white curly wigs. At the far end of the room stood a massive fireplace with a mahogany and marble mantel. Above the mantel was an oil painting of Marty and Kristof when Kristof was probably about eight. If memory served Nikki correctly, that would've been only a couple of years after his mother left the household.

There were other oil-painted portraits on the wall and as Nikki scanned them she was sure she found the one of Ben Waltman, Sara's grandfather—the bastard geezer. Looking at the portrait Nikki could see that Ben didn't appear to be a happy man, with an almost turned-down lip, a hook nose, long neck, black hair, and coal-colored eyes that made Nikki gasp. She could've sworn those eyes were staring at her. It was unnerving.

"Hello," a woman's voice from behind her echoed off the walls in the room.

Nikki jumped and dropped her cracker and cheese onto the Oriental rug that lay atop the walnut hardwood floor. She scooped the scrap into her hand and stood up. Pamela Leiland entered the room looking as gazelle-like as always, with her dark hair slicked back into a long ponytail. She wore a white one-piece jumpsuit which tied into a halter in the back, revealing quite a bit of cleavage. Apparently the Waltmans *did* dress for dinner. Pamela's flawless skin reminded Nikki to continue wearing sunscreen daily. The amazing thing was the woman was so beautiful that she only wore a hint of lip gloss and possibly some pale pink blush.

Pamela extended her arm and manicured hand out to Nikki. In the other hand she held a glass of champagne. "Nikki Sands, isn't it?"

Nikki nodded. "Yes."

"I know we've bumped into each other before and I saw you, I think, over at Grapes having lunch with Isabel the day before the wedding, but we haven't formally met. My apologies. I'm Pamela Leiland. Please sit down. Can I get you anything to drink? Some wine, tea, water?"

"No, thank you." Pamela had definitely settled right into the Waltman Castle without a hitch. She was running this place like the mistress of the manor.

"Marty will be in momentarily and I believe Kristof might try and join us this evening. He's still quite depressed over Susan." Pamela sat down in a velvet wing backed chair.

"He must be."

"We all are. It's been very difficult. I'm still in a state of shock. I suppose that explains the formalities and the champagne and continuing to do everything the way Susan would have done them, or would be doing them right now."

"I don't know if I understand."

Pamela brought her hand up to a diamond necklace around her neck and nervously toyed with it. "You have a best friend, I'm sure. You seem like a nice woman. Someone who probably has a lot of friends."

Nikki shrugged. She didn't know about the plethora of

pals, but she did have a best friend who was now in jail for a murder she didn't commit.

"Susan was my best friend. We had been for years. I loved her like a sister, a lot more than her real sister." Pamela smirked. "There's this part of me that keeps saying that she's just on a vacation, one of her jaunts to a new spa, and that she'll be back. I keep thinking, God, if I go about my day the way I would normally, then maybe she'll come waltzing in."

"Denial."

"Yes, I suppose," Pamela whispered, and reached for a tissue off the table beside her and dabbed at her cheeks and eyes.

"It must be hard. I am so sorry, especially since you lost your husband only a year ago."

Pamela's pale face went alabaster at this comment.

"Antoine Ferrino. You were married to him. Weren't you?"

Pamela nodded slowly. "I was, and it has been hard. Antoine was a very good man and I loved him deeply."

"I'm sure you did." Nikki would have to tiptoe around this one, but she had questions to ask. Either Pamela Leiland was one helluva an actress or she truly was in mourning for her friend. The thing bugging Nikki was Pamela's attitude. She was indeed playing lady of the house, and it didn't totally ring true. She knew how Sara Waltman felt about Susan. Wouldn't she feel that same way about Pamela? The woman had to be the second of a two peas in a pod couple—money-hungry gold diggers. Or was Pamela's friendship with Susan based on that old adage about opposites attracting? "You seem pretty close to Marty."

Once again, the eye dabbing with the tissue. "I didn't expect to fall for Marty. Not at all. I obviously met him through Susan and Kristof and we connected. He's actually been very healing and helpful for me." She lowered her eyes and voice. "He's not Antoine. Antoine was the love of my life, but I know I need to move on. That's what Antoine would've wanted and that's what I'm trying to do and Marty is trying to help me. Now with Susan being gone, I don't know. I can't go back to the city right now. Susan and I shared a condominium near the embarcadero before she made the move out here. There's still so much of her in the condo that I don't feel like I can go back there. Not yet. Jennifer, her sister, is there now."

Nikki wanted to ask Pamela more about Jennifer, but Marty entered the room with Sara draped on one arm and a bottle of wine in his other hand.

"Well, Nikki. How nice to see you. It's not our best moment in time, but your company is always a pleasure."

"Thank you, Marty. I came by to give the family my condolences. I'm not certain I can make it to the services tomorrow."

"That's understandable. Would you stay and have dinner with us?"

"Oh, no, thank you."

"You will stay for some hors d'oeuvres, young lady, and tell us all about how you solved that murder last year over at the Malveaux place," Sara insisted.

Nikki really didn't want to travel down that road again. She hadn't solved anything, the answers from Gabriel's murder had fallen into her lap, and she hated when people glorified her.

Marty must've sensed her uneasiness. "Leave her alone, Aunt Sara. You read all about it in the papers. I'm sure she's had her fill of that bad business. Besides, who wants to talk about murder at a time like this, after what's happened here?"

Sara wobbled over to the sofa that Nikki was seated on and planted herself next to her. "I do."

"Of course you do," Marty interrupted. "She loves mysteries, even tried her hand at writing them years ago. They weren't half bad either. Agatha Christie–type, but a bit more *contemporary*."

"Contemporary?" Sara said. "Marty, is that your word for sexy? If so, it sucks. I wrote some damn good sex scenes and told a good tale. I only published two of the books and then the publisher went kaput and I stopped writing. Took the wind right out of my sails."

"Really? Do you have any copies?" Nikki asked, amused.

"Go upstairs into my room, Marty, and get one from the library."

Marty did as his aunt ordered and a few minutes later he was back with a worn, torn paperback.

"Van Waltman?" Nikki asked running her finger across the name on the cover.

"My publisher thought that writing under a man's name in those days might garner me more fans. Dumb shit. Should've kept my own name. You read it and tell me what you think."

"Aunt Sara, eventually we'll have to wash your mouth out with soap," Marty said.

The ninety-year-old Sara gave him the finger.

"I will." Nikki thanked them and excused herself.

Pamela and Sara said goodbye and Nikki didn't think she got the same vibe coming from Sara toward Pamela that she had about Susan. However, maybe they were being civil for the guest. Nikki doubted it. Sara Waltman did not appear to be the type to bite her tongue about anything or anyone.

"I heard that Isabel Fernandez was arrested for Susan's murder," Marty said when they reached the door. "I know that you two are friends. I really hope she didn't kill Susan."

"Marty, I can assure you that Isabel did not murder Susan."

"She does appear to be a nice woman. I'd hate to think that was the case. I know Susan could be terrible to people. Pamela and I have discussed it, but she also had a charming, sweet side to her. That was the side my son fell in love with, and, frankly, so did we as a family. If your friend Isabel didn't do it, I hope they find out who did."

"They will." Nikki wanted to tell him that actually she would find the killer, but knew how that might sound. She waved the paperback at him and started to walk to her car. She couldn't help wondering about his last statement about the family loving Susan, especially since Nikki knew for a fact that there was one Waltman family member who felt no love lost for Susan.

Chapter 12

Nikki was rounding the shrubbery in front of the Waltman Castle on her way to her car, when she heard a faint sound beyond the bushes. Dusk was setting in and the backdrop of the darkening sky behind the Gothic castle sent her adrenaline into speed zone. The place was kinda spooky in that lighting and the tale of Ben Waltman had a haunting effect at that particular moment. He of the dark eyes that looked to be watching her inside the castle sitting room. It didn't help knowing that a murder had taken place on the grounds only days earlier.

Her mind was quickly put at ease about ghosts and lurking murderers, when she heard quiet laughter followed by more sounds of movement beyond the bushes. Curiosity grabbed hold and Nikki needed to take a peek. She crept over to the hedge and eased down so that she could look through to the goings on at the pool. Well, now, what did we have here? A little rendezvous poolside? Kristof and

Deirdre playing footsie in the Jacuzzi and drinking champagne. Shameful. Nikki's stomach churned with nausea. Two exes making eyes at each other only days after the bride's murder, did not, in her book, bode well.

She inched herself forward to get a bit closer, trying to remain in the shadows of the trees. What were they talking about?

Nikki thought she heard Deirdre saying something about how in time it'd be all right. What did she mean? That he would get over Susan? That in time it would be okay for them to show that they're together again? That in time, they'd definitely be free from being suspected of murder, because poor Isabel would fry for killing the bride?

Damn. The pool pump came on, making it impossible to hear them at all any longer. Only their body language to work with now. They weren't exactly playing footsie like she thought at first. They were seated on opposite ends of the Jacuzzi, across from each other. *But,* they were drinking champagne. Odd choice of drinks, considering. Hell, for that matter, everyone at the Waltman Castle was drinking champagne, and the only one who sort of came up with an excuse for it was Pamela. This was getting stranger by the minute. Was Deirdre's ploy about getting Kristof back into her life? Or was her motive about revenge? The old saying about a woman scorned flashed through Nikki's mind. Could Miss All-American Pie have set out to get even with the newlyweds? Maybe she had plans to take Kristof out, too. Or maybe, she had plans of wheedling her way back into his life and getting her hands on the Waltman loot. Whatever the reasons those two were spending time hot tubbing together, it made Nikki strongly second guess either one of them as innocent.

If Deirdre wanted to get hot and heavy again with Kristof rather than get even, did she kill Susan to get her out of the way and frame Isabel, knowing how brutally Susan had treated Isabel? Or did Deirdre know about Kristof and Isabel's fling and saw an opportunity to get both Susan and Isabel out of the picture?

She *had* to get closer and hear what they were saying. The pool pump turned off and Nikki made it around to the pool house, only feet away from where the Jacuzzi was.

"I can't believe that Isabel Fernandez could be guilty of murder," Deirdre said. "I don't really know her, but I've been in her restaurant and she was a sweet lady."

"I don't know her very well either," Kristof remarked.

What a liar.

"But I can't imagine her killing Susan either. I don't want to believe it. Had I thought anyone could've murdered Susan, it would've been her sister, Jennifer. From the time she showed up here the other day to even after Susan was found, she bad-mouthed her sister and gave Susan nothing but grief," Kristof said. "But the police say that they have some good evidence against Isabel."

"I noticed that Jennifer and Susan didn't seem to get along too well. What was that all about?"

"I asked Susan, but she said that their relationship has always been strained. The two of them didn't grow up in the best situation and Susan made her success on her own. I wonder if Jennifer is in Susan's will? God, I don't know if Susan even had a will. We never talked about those things. Why would we? We had a future together. That's what we talked about."

"Did Jennifer's boyfriend go back to the city with her?"

"That goof, Paulo? Yeah, he's there at the condo with her. I hate to think of them going through Susan's things, but neither Pamela nor I can think of going there right now. I can barely go through her things that are here."

Deirdre slinked closer to Kristof. "I'll do it for you. Whatever you need. I'll do it."

"You've been so good to me, and after everything that has happened between us."

Deirdre set her champagne flute on the side of the Jacuzzi and put her palms on Kritsof's cheeks. "That's all in the past." She kissed him on the forehead. "As I said, I'll do anything you want."

Nikki leaned against the pool house wall. Would Deirdre also do anything possible to get him back into her life?

Deirdre stepped out of the pool and wrapped a towel around herself. "I'd better go. I know it's dinnertime, and your family will start to wonder where you are."

"Won't you stay for dinner? I feel so awkward around everyone right now. Like all eyes are on me."

"I want to. I really do, but it might not look right. I think I should go home." She leaned down and kissed him again, this time on the cheek.

Nikki decided now was a good time to make her exit. She skirted around to her car, a lot of questions spinning in her mind. As she went to open the door, she felt the heaviness of a large hand on her shoulder and she swung around, frightened and ready to go Jennifer Garner a la *Alias* on whoever it was.

"You scared me," she said seeing Marty there.

"I'm sorry. I certainly didn't mean to. I thought you had already left. Then I saw your car still here when I came out to make sure I'd put my Rolls in the garage. It's the one car I have to make sure is in at night."

"I understand." Nikki shifted from one foot to the other. Something about Marty Waltman at that moment didn't feel right. He was looking at her in a strange manner, eyes kind of bugged out, intense, a smirk forming at the edge of his lips. Maybe he'd had a few too many already. The goose bumps sliding down her arms caused her to rub them up and down. She really wanted to get in her car and high-tail it outta there.

"Were you out for a walk?" Marty asked.

"Actually, yes, I was. It's such a beautiful piece of property, and I thought it would be a lovely time of night, and that I would take a stroll." She could hear the tremor in her voice, and that it had crept up an octave.

"I would've shown you around. There are lots of interesting facts about the vineyard, and then, of course, the winery is just up the hill. I enjoy showing off where the finest wines in the region are made."

"I didn't want to bother you."

"It wouldn't have been a bother, Nikki. Did you check out the pool? I believe my caretaker turned the waterfalls on earlier this evening. It's quite gorgeous at night."

Nikki placed a hand on her hip and clucked her tongue. Waving a finger at him. "You know, I missed the pool. I simply love the vines. That was what I wanted to look at."

"Next time you're over, you should come see the pool, maybe take a swim. I keep it heated year round." He sighed, crossed his arms in front of him and rocked back on his heels. "Kristof loves the pool and swimming. He has ever since he was a small boy. I'm so worried about him right now. He's suffered a great loss."

"It is tragic. He's lucky to have a supportive father and family."

Marty's glasses caught the last rays of sun, shadowing them, making it impossible for Nikki to see his eyes behind the lenses.

"There isn't a thing I wouldn't do for my son. He had some difficulties during his childhood and I've made it my job to ensure his happiness."

"As I said, he's very lucky."

"I don't know about luck. It's a parent's love. I love him dearly. He's a good son and he deserves the best. I'd never want to see anything get in the way of him getting all that he deserves, especially now, after he's lost the love of his life. Exactly like you deserve the best. You've been fortunate to find such a wonderful job with Malveaux. Derek is a very good man. You're also lucky that after the fiasco last November and the time you put into snooping around to find Gabriel's murderer, that it didn't get you killed. If I remember right, you were in a very dangerous situation. Very lucky."

"I was, but I'm obviously okay." There was a ring to Marty's words that almost sounded like an offbeat threat.

"That's fortunate. I'm pleased you were so careful not to get hurt. Solving a murder should really be left up to the police. But I can understand curiosity. Like my aunt— always curious about life, people, things that are none of her business. She forgets the old saying sometimes that 'curiosity killed the cat.'"

Nikki glanced at her watch, even though she couldn't read it in the descending darkness. "That's my nature. Curious as a cat. Thanks again for everything. I've got to go."

"Take care, Nikki. Stop by for that swim any time."

"Will do."

Marty opened her car door for her and shut it as she started the engine, her hand on the keys shaking. She couldn't help feeling unnerved. She waved goodbye and drove out of the Waltman property.

Marty's words echoed in her mind on her drive home, disturbing her to the core. He wanted the best for his son. Had he decided that Susan wasn't the best for Kristof? Especially if he'd seen those incriminating photos of her and Blake Sorgensen. Thinking of Blake, Nikki with one hand on the wheel, punched in his number from memory now, for the dozenth time since Isabel's arrest. He must have still been hanging out on his yacht in Cabo. She needed to talk with him, gauge his remorse, and get to the bottom of the affair the two of them obviously had. He didn't pick up the phone, it was only his answering machine, and this was not something she wanted to leave a recorded message about.

She flipped shut her phone, disappointed again that she hadn't reached Blake. That fact struck a chord with her. He had left the reception in a hurry to go off to his yacht in Cabo. Interesting timing. What if he hadn't been as drunk as she'd assumed at the reception? What if his excuse about going to Cabo was simply that—an excuse? What if it was a story to tell, to keep him from being a suspect in Susan's murder? Could he have given Susan the poison and taken off for Mexico with the plan of not returning? Wow, this was getting crazier with each layer Nikki pulled away.

She had no control over where Blake Sorgensen was and she knew she couldn't sit by and wait for him to return from Cabo San Lucas, especially when she had a handful of people she considered suspects in Susan's murder.

And on that list of suspects was Marty Waltman. Nikki went back to reflecting on him and his strange behavior. Had Kristof's dad, on the spur of the moment, decided to murder his new daughter-in-law to ensure that she wouldn't be able to bring Kristof down, or get her hands on the family fortune? More disturbing than his words was the tone he'd used with Nikki. Had he known she'd spied upon Deirdre and Kristof in the pool? Maybe he suspected that her mind churned with doubts about Kristof's undying love for his murdered bride. Could Marty be pleased to see Deirdre and Kristof spending time together again? Maybe he knew that Deirdre's deep hatred for Susan had unleashed a killer in her. If so, was Marty Waltman telling Nikki to back off in order to protect Deirdre and Kristof? Was it his aim to put fear in her? So many unanswered questions. She felt like she was twirling deeper into a black hole. On top of the confusion from unanswered questions, she was also feeling fear, because dammit if Marty Waltman hadn't put a little in her moments earlier. Afraid or not of the Waltman clan, the last thing Nikki was going to do was back off.

Chapter 13

Nikki arrived back at her place just as a full moon rose high above the Mayacamas, lighting the vineyard in an near-ethereal glow. She had plans to make.

The Waltmans and company had done a fine job of creeping her out, and she felt like there were a handful of folks over in Sonoma with some type of motive in seeing Susan dead. But after her fact-gathering evening, she also knew there were a couple more people she needed to see, and those people were in the city.

She checked her answering machine and there was a message from Derek. His voice alone put a smile on her face. Her elation quickly subsided as his tone sounded a wee bit on the cold side.

"Hi, Nikki. It's Derek. I'm afraid I'll have to cancel our dinner appointment for tomorrow night. Something else has come up."

What was that all about? Dinner appointment? Whoever

called it a "dinner appointment," unless it was *all* business, and they had never been just all business. Plus, they'd agreed there was no need for the accountant to join them. The formalities of spelling out who he was on the message? He sounded so distant, almost angry with her. What had she done? Maybe nothing at all and she was being paranoid for no reason.

Not one to wait around and find out if someone was upset with her, she pulled her knit sweater back on and took the short walk over to Derek's place. Ollie greeted her at the front door, wiggling his body incessantly. She bent down to pet the massive Rhodesian Ridgeback. "I've missed you, big boy," she said. "You don't come see me like you used to. Maybe tomorrow I can swing by and we'll go for a run." Ollie licked her hand as if he understood her words.

The front door opened. Nikki looked up to see Derek in sweatpants and worn tee. Something about him like that, looking almost boyish, sent the spine-tingling good kind of willies down her back. "Hi."

"Hello. I thought I heard someone."

"Who's there?" Simon called out in the background.

Nikki arched an eyebrow. "The Boys of Summer are hanging out here?" Quite a twist, considering Derek and his half brother Simon weren't exactly close, and Marco, Simon's boyfriend, was nothing less than a royal pain in the rear.

"Marco has actually designed a decent ad campaign for the winery and asked if I'd take a look."

He was still being way too formal, and acting way too weird.

"Is that Goldilocks? Come on in," Marco hollered out in his Italian accent.

Derek hesitated before swinging the door open. It made her pause, too, before she walked in. Those vibes she was feeling directed at her were nasty and angry. But the boys did appear sort of happy to see her.

Marco poured her a glass of wine as she walked over to the dining room table where they'd apparently been going over Marco's ad ideas. Derek followed behind her. Nikki took the glass of red, took a sip. After tonight, she was in need and wouldn't turn it down even if the offer came from Marco.

"Getting out of the haute couture business?" she asked.

"Ah," Marco sighed and continued on in his Italian accent. "The world of fashion as you know, is about the materialistic world and around money and who has it and who doesn't, and I am simply tiring of it."

Nikki just about spit the wine across the room. Marco a-materialistic? Now, that was a joke.

Simon sidled up next to her. "We told you we've been reflecting on our lives after doing the Zen thing, and our growth is amazing. Marco wants to expand his horizons and since he truly is an artiste, what better for him than to think of Malveaux and the family business?"

"Yes, that is very true," Marco said. "Guru Sansibaba, who we studied with at the spa in magnificent Sedona, says that the God within us is caused by the God outside of us. This is the reflection of all that we do, and all that others do, and we are one microcosm of the macrocosm. One tiny cell in a larger one. By thinking blindly about riches and speaking ugly of others, we are only harming ourselves."

"Mhhm. Guru Sansibaba, such an intelligent man," Simon chimed in.

Oh, brother. Nikki wondered if Derek could read through these two as clearly as she could. After Gabriel's murder last fall, Derek had basically given them the boot for their part in everything. They'd tried desperately to run Nikki off the vineyard, afraid that she might be after what they were after—the Malveaux fortune. She wasn't buying into the idea that some guru at a spa in Sedona had turned these two into spiritual, loving beings.

"My suggestion with a new ad campaign is intelligent and filled with amore. I am making a suggestion to Derek that the winery incorporate the concept of Zen into their ads. It is all about peace and love, and what a grand idea to associate it with a vineyard. Guru Sansibaba says that what grows in the ground can only be ripened through love and nourishment. That said, there is much love at Malveaux Estate." He winked at Nikki, then shot a glance at Derek.

She didn't know what to say. Derek took her by the elbow, and they walked over to the sofa. The boys jabbered on to each other about the spiritual growth they were feeling within themselves and for each other and the brilliance of the guru.

Derek gestured for her to sit down. "I take it this isn't a social visit," he said in that same cold tone he had used on the answering machine.

"I, well . . . Actually, did I do something wrong? Are you upset with me?"

His eyes widened. "Should I be?"

"Not that I can think of. You sounded kind of perturbed with me on the message you left, and I thought I'd ask."

"No. We're fine. As I said something else has come up for me tomorrow night and I can't make our dinner. That's all."

"Oh. I understand." Not really. Usually he'd tell her what had come up or why he couldn't make it. But she was getting nothing. He'd never sounded so abrupt with her. "Did you have a good trip?"

"Fine."

Nikki set her wine glass on the coffee table in front of her. This was going well. "Do you want to reschedule, maybe?"

"I'm not sure of my schedule. My planner is up in the office. We can talk about it next week."

Nikki was going to go out on a limb here, but she was losing ground with him and really wanted to get some traction back before that slight crack in the window she'd noticed at the wedding was nailed shut. "I need to go into the city this weekend and see a friend. Would you like to join me?"

Derek studied her for a moment. "I'm sure there's someone else you'd rather take along."

"No. There isn't. I'm still fairly new around here and haven't been to the city but a few times. When I lived in L.A. I didn't get north often. I could use someone to tour around with me."

"What about your friend that you're going to visit?"

This was dicey because she didn't want to give him any indication about her real reasons for going. However, she did want to stick as close to the truth as possible. "She's not exactly a close friend, more of an acquaintance, really."

"Why are you going into the city to see an acquaintance?" he asked, probably sensing she was up to something.

Now she would have to tell a story. "I think I told you about my interest in writing, after my acting career failed."

He nodded.

"And, obviously, you know I love a good mystery."

"A little too much," he replied.

"Right. Anyway, this gal has information that could help me write a mystery."

"Like a writing instructor?"

At least he was opening up to her, but she could hear the skepticism in his voice. "Yeah, kind of like that."

"Uh, huh. Do you plan on pursuing a writing career, Nikki, or do you want to sell wine?"

Ooh, she'd assumed too quickly that he'd changed his tone with her. "Of course I want to sell wines. I love my job." How could he doubt her about that? She'd thrown herself into learning everything about wines, winemaking, grapes, all of it from the seed on up. He knew that. "The writing thing is a hobby, that's all. Now, I'd really like you to come to San Francisco with me."

"Excuse me, oh *excuse me,* did I hear someone mention San Francisco?" Simon said.

Derek turned his head towards the boys at the dining room table who had obviously been eavesdropping, feigning to be fawning over their new idea and artwork. "Nikki is going into the city to talk with a woman about mystery writing," Derek said, his voice strained. "She's looking for a tour guide."

Simon and Marco's eyes both lit up. "Well, Goldilocks, you've come to the right place," Simon said.

"Marvelous, *Bellisima.* We'll take you around the wild city, and we'll have a—how do you say—'a really good time' in English?" Marco replied.

"Blast, darling. We'll have a blast," Simon instructed his lover. "Good timing, too. I was starting to feel a bit bored here on the vineyard. There's a darling Japanese man there on Kansas Street that Marco and I must go see. We're really looking to go feng shui style. Guru Sansibaba says that home decor, especially feng shui, can help bring in the right vibrations for a spiritually profitable life. Vibrations are what connects all of us, in the one energy sphere. What a lovely idea, Goldilocks. We would love to accompany you."

"Oh, no, that's okay," she protested and looked to Derek to save her from this onslaught. However, he appeared to be almost enjoying it, with what could only be construed as an amused smile on his face.

"We would be delighted to take you," Marco said.

"Yes, of course. Who better than a couple of queens to show you around the kingdom of queendom?" Simon said. The Boys of Summer broke into simultaneous laughter.

Nikki didn't laugh as a sinking feeling set into her stomach.

"That settles it, when you get off work tomorrow head on up to the mansion and we'll set out," Simon ordered. "Maybe I can get us a dinner reservation at the Big 4 Restaurant on Nob Hill."

"Oh, yes, that would be splendid," Marco said and clapped his hands together. "And we have to, *have* to stay at The Clift. It's a must, so divine. Our treat. It's important that those of us who have monetary gain, share with the less fortunate."

"Super." She swigged back the wine and stood up. "I need to get going. Thanks for the vino." She could hear *the edge* in her own voice now, and wondered what she could have done to Derek to start this pissing contest? Because now she was involved in it and not by choice. At that moment she wasn't at all happy with the man of her dreams.

As she closed the door behind her and started to walk back to her place, a cool wind slapped her slightly across the face. Whether it was the chill traveling through her or the light bulb in her brain finally flickering to light, Nikki had a thought. The car the other night. When Andrés had brought her home from dinner in Sonoma with Deirdre. She smacked herself on the forehead. Duh. It had to have been the boys who'd sped on past and then reported in to Derek that they'd seen her with Andrés. How would she patch this one up? It wasn't like he was going to admit that he might be jealous. Hell, she wasn't even sure if that was the case. Turn around and go back to his place and say, "Oh, by the way, I didn't have dinner with Andrés the other night, he just brought me home. It's you I want."

She made it back to her place, flopped down on the couch, and used her remote to turn on the TV. TLC was playing an oldie-but-goodie—*When Harry Met Sally.* Perfect.

There was a part of her that wanted to go back to Derek and tell him about the other night, make it clear to him that she wanted to be with him, as unprofessional and desperate as it might sound. But there was also a little part inside her that couldn't help wondering what Andrés was up to at that moment.

Chapter 14

Friday morning before work, Nikki packed for the weekend and then went to see Isabel as soon as visiting hours
began. Her dear friend sat opposite her on the other side of
a glass partition wearing a sad expression. Simultaneously,
Isabel and Nikki picked up their phones so they could
speak with each other. Deep lines across Isabel's young
face had formed in a matter of a couple of days, and her
eyes were sunken with dark circles framing them.

"I'm going to get you out of here," Nikki promised.

Isabel nodded and gave her a pathetic attempt at a smile.
"They think that I gave Susan a vial of that poison and told
her it was cocaine."

"What? Why would they think that?" Nikki asked,
shocked to hear this turn of events. She knew that the cops
thought Isabel had poisoned Susan, but she was under the
assumption that since Isabel had catered the event that the
police thought Isabel had put the poison in the food or wine.

"There is rumor that someone on the catering staff heard Susan say to me that she needed a pick-me-up, and that I supplied that for her."

"Did Susan say anything like that to you?" Nikki asked.

"I cannot remember anything like that. It is possible. If she did, she said it in passing and I did not take it to mean for real. I was so busy that day. You saw me. If she did say something to me about needing some energy, I would have thought she was asking for coffee, not drugs."

Nikki pondered all of this for a moment, remembering standing in the foyer at the Waltman Castle shortly after the coroner had taken Susan's body away. Susan's sister Jennifer had brought up the fact that her sister liked to dabble in recreational drugs once in a while, and Pamela hadn't denied it. But why would the police think that Isabel provided it? Yes, they claimed to have found the vial of sodium fluoroacetate in Isabel's truck, but it wasn't as if Susan and Isabel were bosom buddies. Nikki doubted that if Susan wanted a toot, she'd go to the caterer she treated as a lowly servant. She brought this point up to Isabel, whose eyes glossed over.

"Nikki, there is something that I have never told to you. It is something I am so ashamed of."

"There is nothing you need to be ashamed of around me."

Isabel sighed. "When I first come into this country I was a little more wild. I knew how to party, and I liked to forget my troubles. Things were hard for me after my mother passed and I moved here, though I was going to be here with my brother and there were so many possibilities, I was stupid. I thought the best way to make friends was to throw good parties. One night after moving here, I had people over and there were drugs. My brother heard about it and he told me that if I did not change that I would have to go back to Spain. Since the vineyard owners of Spaniard's Crest helped to finance the restaurant and I knew that my brother was serious with me, I paid attention. I have never had anything to do with drugs since that night."

"But there are still some people out there who like to talk trash and this murder has stirred up the gossip again."

"Yes," Isabel whispered into the phone.

It was an ugly mess, but Nikki was more determined than ever to wade through it and get to the bottom of all of it. She needed to find out which worker had mentioned to the police about overhearing Susan say to Isabel that she needed a pick-me-up. On that train of thought, she reflected on the young man working that night who Susan had belittled in front of a slew of people. What was his name again? How could she forget? It was the reason Susan jabbed at him. It was Louis Faulker. When Nikki made it back to Sonoma on Sunday, she'd track him down.

"Do you have a roster of people who worked for you that night?" Nikki asked.

"It should be in my office inside my desk. Why?"

"I'd like to see who was working and maybe ask some questions."

"Is that a good idea? I do not want you to get into any trouble on my account."

"Listen to me, Isabel. I don't want to paint an ugly picture, but I think you know how much trouble you are in."

Isabel's eyes watered over again as she nodded in response.

"That said, the police seem pretty focused on blaming you for this and finding a way to convict you. Andrés and I think you were framed."

Isabel's eyes widened as she absorbed this thought. "But why? I do not think I have any enemies. The only person who never seemed to care for me was Susan Jennings."

"Exactly. I don't think that whoever is framing you did it because they have a grudge against you. I think you are the easy fall guy."

Isabel looked confused.

"Because of the way Susan treated you, and in front of others with no holding back, it made the killer see you as an easy target to blame so that there would be no suspicion on him or her."

"And you are trying to find out who this person is?"

"Yes."

"No, Nikki. You cannot put your life in that kind of risk for me. The truth will come out."

"Don't be naïve, my friend. Yes, the truth will come out, and I'll find out the truth. I'm fine. I know what I'm doing." Although she said it, she couldn't help wonder in the back of her mind if she really felt it, but she had to give Isabel some hope. "You know and I know that you would do the same for me."

Isabel placed a hand on the glass partition between them, Nikki met Isabel's hand with her own. Isabel mouthed the words "thank you." Both women couldn't hold back their tears any longer. "Please be careful," Isabel said.

"I will."

Their time was up. They said goodbye to each other and Nikki headed back to the vineyard for the day's work. On her way she stopped off at Grapes. Isabel's manager, Carmen, was there. She explained to her that Isabel needed her to retrieve something from her desk. Carmen didn't question her, knowing that the two women were close friends. Nikki found the roster right where Isabel instructed. She scrolled down the list of about twenty people and found Louis Faulker's name. On her way back to Malveaux Estate, she called Louis's number on her cell.

A man answered. When Nikki asked for Louis, she got quite a surprise.

"Lou? Nah. He split," the man said.

"Split?"

"Yeah, you know like later. I came home Sunday after the national video game tournament in Sacramento, and the dude just left me a note saying he was moving out. I'm sorta pissed, too, you know, cause the dude owes me cash for the phone bill, and the rent's due."

"Right. Do you know where he went?"

"Like, no. He's a weird dude. Kinda sketchy."

"Sketchy, how?"

"You know, sketchy, like moody, freaky. Who is this, anyway?"

"No one. Thanks." Nikki flipped shut her phone. This was not looking good for Louis. The guy leaves town the day after Susan's murder. She belittled him at the reception, and on top of it his roommate thought he was strange? It didn't make him a killer. There were a lot of strange people around. Nikki would have to be sure and see what she could do about tracking Louis down after she returned from the city.

There was a lot of work to be done at the winery, and it made the day go by fast. Before she knew it, she was scrunched into the back seat of the boys' Porsche.

Nikki had to admit that the hour into San Francisco was amusing, even with the added memorized quotes of the Guru Sansibaba pouring out of the boys. It still bothered her that Derek had been so cold and off toward her and she still wanted to set things straight with him. She'd hoped to do so before leaving, but he hadn't been around the winery all day. She had no idea what she was going to say to him, but something did need to be said. It would have to wait.

She had to discover the truth about Susan and who had murdered her. She had to see Isabel set free.

Simon cranked up the stereo to Frankie Goes to Hollywood and sang along with old Frankie. Marco looked at his partner behind the wheel, totally mesmerized. Nikki could see why. Like Derek, Simon had golden hair, only he wore his longer than his half brother, and it stirred wildly in the wind with the top down on the convertible. He had cheekbones that looked to be etched out of stone and his sea-green eyes, although deeper set than Derek's, still captivated. Marco and Simon made a statement about handsome looks when they entered a room.

Marco was the counterpart to Simon's Scandinavian and Irish descent, as the Italian man played every bit of the dark, sometimes brooding, eccentric lover. Nikki would've never guessed after the way they'd treated her less than a year earlier that she'd be riding in a car with them on their way to San Francisco. She knew at some point she'd have to lose the two of them, even if it was only for a couple of hours, so she could really do what she came here for.

Simon heaved an exaggerated sigh once Frankie's song was over. He tossed his blond tendrils out of his eyes after setting his sunglasses off of his face to hold back the blowing hair. Nikki could've sworn there were tears in his eyes as he took Marco's hand.

"I love that song. So many memories, so much fun."

Marco nodded. "Remember though, love, that Guru Sansibaba says that memories are only a reflection of time, and that living in the present is where real love is made."

Nikki slumped back in the seat and tightened her scarf around her hair, hoping to keep it somewhat tamed. She had fine hair that if mussed at all would wind up looking like either a bird's nest or a stringy mess. Neither one she desired.

"Goldilocks?" Simon said.

By now she'd gotten used to their pet name for her and had pretty much stopped cringing every time they uttered it. She responded with a "yes," wondering if they even remembered her real name.

"I was thinking that I really do like your style. You know how to juggle an act or two, don't you?"

Marco glanced at Simon. Whatever this was about these two had already gone rounds with it, and she wasn't sure she wanted to see where this was going to go, because she didn't even know what in the hell Simon was referring to. But hey, between Frankie Goes to Hollywood and Streisand's *Evergreen* CD, Nikki didn't want to know what those two might pull out of the music case next. She doubted it was Sheryl Crow. So she decided to play along with whatever line of questioning Simon was headed with her.

"Simon, I haven't the faintest idea as to what you're talking about, but I'm certain you're going to enlighten me."

"I like that, too, about you. You're coy and sweet and you know how to *play* naïve. My brother goes for that sort of thing. But Marco and I know that's not your gig. And, I'm thinking that maybe Derek has figured it out, too, and that's why he didn't join you on your jaunt into the city."

Now he had her interested along with kinda ticked off, because if he was insinuating that who she was, was all an act, well he might be really sorry. She was pretty sure she could take Simon on. She certainly never tried to *play* innocent or naïve. In fact, those were the last set of words she'd use to describe herself. Instead of protesting his descriptive words for her, she questioned him. "I'm game. What in the world are you talking about?"

"Quit teasing her, Simon. She is sweet, and I don't think Guru Sansibaba would like the way you're treating a cell in the body of the God of us all, as we are all God, and she is a Goddess."

"Oh, all right. I know I shouldn't be such a cad. Sometimes it's hard not to fall into my old ways. Here's the deal. We were probably bad boys the other night, listening to your conversation with my big brother. But I knew when you asked him to join you, that he wasn't going to take you up on your offer, and, well, Marco and I couldn't refuse a trip into San Francisco. Speaking of, there's the Golden Gate." Simon pointed to the bridge, which on any other day would've taken Nikki's breath away, but she was too intent on Simon's words to take a real good look at the city's icon.

"Simon, would you like to tell me what you're talking about?" She leaned into the back of the driver's seat, getting closer to Simon in the hopes of hearing him better over the wind.

"The other night, Marco and I took Derek out to dinner. That was the night *you two* were supposed to have dinner together. He came home looking worn. We were out on our evening walk, when we saw him come in."

"We decided to see if he was doing okay," Marco said. "It's a part of the outreach mission the Guru . . ."

"I know, Sansibaba," she replied cutting him short, not wanting to hear any more idioms the Guru had shared with the boys for at least the next twenty years.

"Yes. We really are trying to make improvements on ourselves and our relationships with family and friends. One step at a time, though. I'm simply pleased my mother hasn't returned from gallivanting across the country to every known spa in the western hemisphere. It's only too bad that she isn't open enough to experience the Greater Healing Spa of Sedona."

There was something Nikki and Simon could agree on. Patrice's presence was certainly not missed.

"We also wanted to tell Derek our ideas for selling the wines that night," Marco said.

"True. We offered to take him out and he finally agreed to go have dinner with us. On our drive back into the estate, we were maybe giving him a hard time about you," Simon said.

Marco giggled. "I think she does that just beautifully by herself."

Simon playfully slapped Marco's knee. "Or she used to, anyway."

Nikki's face heated into a burn.

Marco turned around and saw her. "I'm sorry. Don't be mad. We are only playing."

She clenched her fists.

"We thought it would be funny to drop Derek at your door step. He didn't think we were funny either."

"I think we're funny," Marco said. "The Guru might not always think so, but he did say that humor is what lightens our load when we feel the path has become too entrenched with the stress of the physical world."

These two were driving her batty at this point and now she was wishing they'd pop another frigging CD into the player, even if it *was* Liza, Streisand, or Cher, for that matter.

"When we turned the corner to go to your cottage and push my brother out of the car, we saw you climbing the stairs with that absolutely divine creature—mmhmm, Andrés Fernandez."

"Hey," Marco protested.

Simon took his hand again. "Oh, baby, you can look, just don't order off the menu."

"Whatever."

"What does me being with Andrés have to do with anything?" Nikki asked. She was right. Derek thought she'd been out with Andrés and had traded in his offer for dinner out with him to be with Andrés. She wanted to hear this from the boys, though, just to confirm her thoughts.

"It has everything to do with anything. Don't you get it, Goldilocks? Derek and you have this silly flirtation going on, we thought he should take it to the next step, but . . ."

"Now he won't, because he thinks you're dating Andrés," Marco said.

"I'm not dating Andrés. For goodness' sakes, the only reason he was with me was because I needed a ride home from a dinner I had, and not with him, I might add. Then, I spent time talking with him because his sister, Isabel, who is my good friend, as Andrés is, was arrested for murdering Susan Jennings."

"Yes, we heard about that. Ugly, ugly business. How do you get yourself tangled up in these things, Goldilocks?" Simon asked.

"Isabel didn't kill anyone, and I am not dating Andrés."

"Hmmm. Okay. Maybe you should tell it to the boss man."

Nikki leaned back in the seat of the car. What a mess. But on the flipside, the Boys of Summer did seem to believe that Derek reciprocated her feelings for him, so maybe talking to him about it would be easier than she thought. Hell, it wasn't going to be easy no matter what, but she couldn't help but smile for a second. She needed to do damage control. Bite the bullet and talk to Derek—about everything. Dating Andrés? Silly notion . . .

She crossed her fingers and hoped she'd find the right words to say to Derek without sounding like a fool. Fat chance of that. But once in the city, and in a place where she could have some privacy, she had to take that chance and call him. Maybe, just maybe, she could lure Derek to the city after all, question the handful of suspects on her list, and, ultimately, kill two birds with one stone.

Chapter 15

Nikki and the boys checked into The Clift, and, luckily, Simon and Marco wanted some alone time. She agreed to meet up with them later in the lobby for a glass of wine and "an evening out on the town." To the boys that meant starting around eight. No idea what could be in store with that, but she was determined to go with it. That was just in case her phone call to Derek didn't work. She really needed a glass of wine before dialing his number. A little liquid courage could come in handy at that moment, but more than that, she needed a clear head, and only had a couple of hours to use it.

She dialed Derek's office number and got his voice mail, then tried his cell with no luck. She sucked it up with the third call and got his answering machine at home. It was after hours at the winery and he wasn't answering any of his numbers. Was he screening his calls? What if he didn't want to talk to her *at all*? She looked at the clock on the side table next to the bed in her room. It was a little after five. He was probably out on his evening walk or having a glass of wine with the staff. Occasionally he hung in there for the employees' nightly ritual of mixing and matching potions to see who had the potential to be the next winemaker. It was a joke among the crew. Nikki didn't participate much, as she liked to get either a walk or another run in before imbibing. Plus she wasn't sure if it was such a good idea to drink every day. The man who she thought was her father for the first seven years of her life made a practice of tippling the bottle daily, and because of it he wound up dead.

She chewed on the side of her lip as Derek's message played out. Then after the beep she went for it. "Hi, Derek, it's me, Nikki. Listen, I think there is a misunderstanding between us about the other night. You know, about dinner. We really need to talk. I would love it if you came into the city tomorrow, and had dinner with me. On me. I mean, I'll pay. I hope you come. We're staying at The Clift. Uh, if you want to meet me, call me on my cell. I'm thinking around seven." The machine ran out of time. Smooth. Real smooth. Nothing like sounding like an idiot, and a desperate one at that. No time to sulk. She had a few more phone calls to make. She needed to speak with Susan's sister Jennifer, and hopefully Blake Sorgensen. The other star in those very risqué photos she'd seen at the Waltman Castle had finally returned from his jaunt to Cabo.

She decided to call Jennifer first, after finding the number listed under Susan's name. Her odds thus far of Blake answering his phone didn't seem to be in her favor.

After the first ring, a woman answered. "Where are you?" she hissed.

"Uh, excuse me?"

"Oh, sorry. I thought you were someone else. I have a date tonight and he's late. *Who's* this?"

"Hi. I'm Nikki Sands and I knew Susan Jennings."

"Who didn't know her? What do you need?"

"Is this Jennifer?"

"Yes? Again, what the hell do you want?"

Nice phone manners. What had Nikki expected? It wasn't as if Jennifer Jennings exuded class the other day at the wedding and thereafter during the police interrogation. "I'm having a hard time with accepting Susan's murder. You see, I also know the woman who has been accused of her murder, and I don't think she did it." Staying as close to the truth as possible. Putting into practice that new motto of hers.

"The police think she did it."

"I understand that, but I'm not so sure. I was wondering if maybe I could come by so that you might answer a few questions for me?"

"Are you like some detective or something?"

Nikki recognized that Jennifer was becoming irritated with her and knew she had to do something quick to keep her on the line. "I'm not a detective. Like I said, I would hate to see an innocent woman go to jail, wouldn't you?"

"No. What? I don't give a rat's ass."

New tactic needed here. "Fine. Indulge me, please. I'll buy you a drink or two."

A sigh came across the phone. "Tell you what, why don't you make your way to my place." She gave her the address on Brannan Street, close to the embarcadero, in the North Beach area. "If I'm still here and Paulo hasn't shown up, maybe I'll go have a drink with you, just so I can get the hell outta here, and then when he does show up and I'm not here, it'll teach him a lesson never to do that to me again."

"I'll be there in ten minutes." Nikki hung up the phone. Her call to Sorgensen would have to wait. She prayed Paulo wouldn't beat her to the punch. She ran a quick

comb through her hair and applied lip gloss. Then jetted
down the stairs and hailed a cab.

Nikki handed the cabbie a ten and didn't wait for any
change when he pulled up a few minutes later near Ghi-
rardelli Square. Susan and Pamela's place was located
around the block from the square, but the cabbie couldn't
park because it was Friday evening and the area was filled
with tourists.

She walked the block and found the building where she
pressed the intercom. Someone had spent some cash to get
into this place, with its complete Victorian charm painted
in a royal blue and trimmed in teal. Nikki couldn't see Susan living here. It was too cool. Pamela, maybe, but Susan?

"Is that you, Paulo?" a voice rang out over the intercom
system.

"No, actually it's me, Nikki Sands."

A minute later the front door swung open. On the other
side stood the woman Nikki remembered as Jennifer Jennings. She wore another slinky dress like the one she had
worn at the wedding, although this one was in fuchsia and
barely covered her ass. If stereotypes proved true in this
case, it was starting to appear as if the Jennings girls were
not exactly raised with much couth, especially Jennifer.

Nikki recalled those few moments at the wedding when
she witnessed the two siblings arguing, and then, watched
as Susan gave her sister a check. Had Jennifer been riding
on her sister's coattails? If so, how much of the money that
Susan was giving her had come from Susan's bank account
versus Kristof's? It wouldn't make a good motive for murder to kill off the goose laying the golden eggs. However,
Nikki also couldn't forget the hatred for Susan in Jennifer's
eyes, followed by the complacency Jennifer seemed to express over her death.

"Come on in. My jerk-off boyfriend still hasn't made it, and I've been calling his freaking cell phone all afternoon. He better have a good excuse is all I have to say, because if he continues to pull this crap with me, I might have to call it quits. Men! You know what I mean, don't you?"

Nikki nodded. Befriending Jennifer was probably going to be the best route to take. "Don't I ever, girlfriend."

Jennifer turned on her four-inch heels that were straight out of a strip club, and raised an eyebrow to her. She turned back around, click-clacking on the walnut hardwoods inlaid with a decorative diamond of pine every third plank. The pattern was gorgeous, and, once inside the living room, the pattern switched with the pine floor being the main wood in the space. Jennifer Jennings was living in style.

Maybe calling her girlfriend wasn't so sharp.

Once inside the main rooms of the house Nikki could see where it reflected Susan—a lot of chrome and black and cream, with fresh purple lilies in a vase on top a black and cream marble coffee table. Susan must've had a lily fetish. The main room opened up into the kitchen, which had to have been great for entertaining purposes.

Jennifer swung open the door on the chrome refrigerator and pulled out a bottle of Stoli from the freezer. "Screw waiting to get to a club for a drink. Maybe the loser will show up by the time we're done."

The kitchen atmosphere was a bit warmer than the living room because of a gorgeous set of cherry cabinets, which were carried all along one wall into a dining area as they scaled down from full cabinets to a book shelf.

Jennifer wagged the vodka at her. "Want some? I need to take the edge off. I'm telling you, if Paulo doesn't get here soon, I'll just about have a shit fit."

Wasn't she already doing that? "No, thanks. Some water might be nice."

"Suit yourself." Jennifer first poured herself a tall glass of the vodka on ice with a splash of club soda, then got a glass of water from the tap for Nikki. Real congenial type. "So, you came here to talk about my sister, huh? What do you want to know?" Jennifer leaned against the kitchen island.

She obviously wasn't going to ask Nikki if she wanted to sit down. Nikki set her water glass down opposite the hostess with the mostest. This was not a welcome visit. "I got the feeling that you and Susan weren't exactly close."

There was a long pause. "You know there was a time, a long time ago when we were really close, but it's funny how time, and money change a person." Jennifer motioned around the condominium.

"You two didn't have money growing up?"

Jennifer laughed and took a big slug of her vodka. "Shit, no. We weren't rich *at all*. I take it you didn't know Susan very well?"

"No. I only saw her a few times," Nikki replied.

"Yeah, well, even if you knew her, she wouldn't have told you the truth about our upbringing."

"You can't be ashamed about where you came from." That was an out and out lie, because shame filled Nikki every time she thought about where she came from. "People can't help that."

"What are you, some Pollyanna type or something? Of course you can be freaking ashamed, but, hell, the truth is the truth, and as much as my sister was an ass, she did do a damn good job of pulling herself up and out. But she had quite a bit of help along the way, unlike some of us."

"What do you mean?"

"You saw my sister, all blonde and tall. Boobs out to here, and boy, did she know how to use everything God or the plastic surgeon had given her to her advantage."

"I take it that it hasn't been so easy for you?"

"Easy? Easy? Ha! No way. It's been hell, but now I'm doing okay." Another glance around the condo.

"Did you inherit this place?"

Another long pause and swig off her drink. "Yeah, big sis finally kicked down for something. It was like pulling teeth to get her to do it, but, you know, who would've thought she would get herself killed? I figured it was a pipe dream that I'd ever have a place like this. I know she wanted to leave it to her bosom buddy, but I convinced her that blood was thicker than water."

"She had a will then?"

"Hell, yes. She had a lot of moolah on her own without that Kristof dude. But a lot was never enough for her, if you know what I mean. She wanted to be the female Trump all the way. I heard that she even tried to pick up on Trump himself in the past, but he was all into that Melania model chick he's married to now. He blew old Sis off like she was nothing. Kinda funny, I think, cause my sister had this the-ory that she could get any man in bed and then empty out his pocketbook. With most men she was right."

"You mentioned her bosom buddy? Are you talking about Pamela Leiland?"

"The one and only. Those two are or were two peas in a pod."

"They knew each other for a while, I take it?" Nikki asked and took a sip of her water.

"I guess. I hadn't seen my sister until like the last six months, when I saw her in a photo in one of those glossy magazines. You know, of the rich and famous, and there she was, all boobs and smiles and willing to die for Kristof Waltman and flashing that humongous diamond ring of hers in the picture. I figured I'd better get my ass out here when I saw that, and congratulate the happy couple in person."

"Where were you living?"

"In a freaking pit in Phoenix, and my sister glamming it up kinda got me thinking that blood is thicker than water, and she was my only living relative, and, well, you know, family shouldn't be so far apart from one another. I told her if she put me on the *payroll* that I would keep my mouth shut about where she really came from. I got the impression that her moneybags new hubby didn't have a clue what she was all about. I know he had an idea there was no money for us growing up, but he didn't know the extent of the story. That much I'm sure of."

Nikki shifted her weight from one foot to the other. She was starting to dislike Jennifer as much as she had Susan. She was an opportunist. Nikki knew that several of her family members could easily become just that if they learned that she was earning a decent figure these days.

The front door slammed, and Jennifer's head snapped around. Nikki turned to see the man who had accompanied Jennifer to the wedding the other day, all tall, muscular, good-looking in a kind of slimy way. Like a greased up Antonio Banderas. His dark eyes were shrouded with a long fringe of lashes. Damn, if he didn't look like he'd just walked straight out of one of The Godfather flicks.

He walked over and lifted Jennifer off her feet. "Hi, love muffin."

That was gross. Love muffin? Eeww.

Jennifer laughed and then suddenly remembered that she was angry with him as she beat her fists into him. "Where the hell have you been?"

"I'm sorry, baby." He kissed her in what some would call a passionate kiss; to Nikki it was nothing short of disgusting. "I was in a meeting with *the boss*, and I told you before how that can go."

The boss. Nikki's mind went into a tailspin as her imagination got carried away with her. What if Jennifer convinced her sister to include her in her will, then the boyfriend, old Paulo, who it sounded like had some kind of mafia connection—for God's sakes, who emphasizes boss the way he just did?—and Jennifer decided to axe Susan and take the plush condo and whatever else they could get their hands on? And, now Nikki was standing right there in the middle of them. What if they turned on her because she was sniffing around? It wasn't like Jennifer had held back any of her feelings toward her sister and the way she'd wormed her way into Susan's will.

Paulo's gaze turned toward Nikki. "Who is this?" he asked in a smarmy way, trying in Nikki's estimation to be charming. Not even on the chart.

"Oh, her? That's Nikki . . ."

Nikki stretched out her hand and Paulo took it in his and kissed it. Double eeww! "Sands." She finished the introduction for Jennifer.

"Yeah, she's got some questions about Susan. She doesn't think that chick they threw in the slammer out in Sonoma did it. She's her friend." Jennifer cocked her head to the side, placed a hand on her jutted out hip, then picked up her glass for a drink of the vodka mix.

Nikki tightened her purse strap over her shoulder. "I think I should probably be heading out. I know you two have plans."

"Wait a minute. Wait a freaking minute," Jennifer said. "What the hell is this?" Nikki watched as Jennifer pointed out lipstick stains on Paulo's white button-down. "You haven't been in a meeting. You've been screwing someone else. I told you, Paulo. I freaking told you that if you pulled that shit again on me then you were a goner, and I freaking mean it. Damn you." She slapped him hard across the face, and turned around, storming out of the room, vodka drink still in hand. "And, by the time I walk back in here, you better be freaking gone!" A slam of the door resounded from the back of the condominium.

Nikki tried to smile at Paulo. This was awkward.

He turned to her. "Don't worry about it. That's nothing. She'll be out in fifteen with a new outfit on, cause I set a present on the bed for her when I first came in. See, I snuck in first, put the present on the bed, and then came back and shut the front door, so she wouldn't know. Now she'll be all giddy, because there is nothing that woman likes more than gifts. She'll forget all about being upset with me. Besides, it was just my secretary giving me a kiss good night, you know, like a friendly kiss on the cheek. Once Jen mellows out, I can explain it to her and she'll get back with the program."

Sure, fella. Whatever. "I really need to get going. Can you tell her that I said goodbye?"

"You don't want to stick around? We'll take you for some dinner. If you've got some questions about Susie, I can probably answer them. I know a thing or two about Miss High and Mighty."

This piqued Nikki's interest, but, dammit, she really wanted to get the hell out of this place with the two wannabe *Sopranos* actors, and move on to her next freak show. Never in a million years would she have thought she would've looked forward to hanging out with the Boys of Summer at a drag queen show, but, by golly, at that moment that sounded like a top-of-the-line option. "That's fine. I have plans for dinner already myself."

"Too bad." He pulled out one of his cards and flipped it to her. "If you change your mind, give me a ring. We can meet up for lunch or something." He winked at her.

"Sure. Maybe I'll do that." Nikki headed for the door and didn't breathe until she'd closed it behind her and headed down towards the square to mix in with the crowd milling around. She wanted to get far away from that condo, because those two inside that place were definitely nutcases, and possibly murderers as well.

Chapter 16

Before heading down to the lobby to meet the boys, Nikki placed another call to Blake Sorgensen. This time, to her surprise, he answered.

"Nikki who?" he asked.

"Sands. From the Waltman wedding. We sat at the same table. I've been trying to reach you for the past few days. It's about Susan's murder."

Nothing.

"Mr. Sorgensen? Are you there?"

"Yes. I'm sorry, but I was unaware of this. I've been out of town for a few days. Did you say that Susan was murdered?"

"I'm sorry. Yes. I'd like to have lunch with you and ask you a few things."

He did sound shocked, and without even asking her why she wanted to ask him anything, he agreed to a lunch date. She hung up and crossed her fingers that he'd show the following afternoon. The fact that he'd returned from Mexico could mean that he wasn't involved with Susan's murder, or maybe it meant that he'd taken his chances and once he'd discovered Isabel had been arrested for the murder, he'd returned from Cabo.

Nikki sighed and put on a pair of khaki slacks and a black knit sweater set and took a look in the floor length mirror. Nope. Way too conservative for the company she'd be keeping tonight. Why not go all Moulin Rouge for Simon and Marco? There was an outfit she'd bought before moving to Napa that was a bit far out from her normal style, but it had been for a party for a trendy new designer in L.A. A rock star's kid gone Donna Karan.

The outfit was pretty cute, with a black silk skirt that pleated into the center, along with a dark rose-pink silk halter blouse that sported embroidery stitched in black and black pearl buttons down the front.

Smiling to herself, she took the outfit up an extra notch with fish net stockings and full makeup. Why she'd brought the fishnets in the first place, she wasn't sure. Some subconscious fantasy that involved the straight Malveaux brother. Subconscious? It was front and center. Instead, she'd be sporting her "Living La Vida Loca" apparel for a couple of gay guys who called her Goldilocks and fed her spiritual tidbits from a man who sounded like he was straight out of Disney's version of *Aladdin*. The boys wouldn't recognize her, and they'd either laugh hysterically or love it.

They loved it so much when she entered the lobby that they gasped and then started clapping.

"Oh, my God, a woman really does exist in there," Simon remarked. "All this time we thought you were only a sweet girl, but look at you."

Marco twirled her around. "Our baby is all grown up.

But how do we know she's really a woman?" He winked at her. "You *do* look wonderful."

She laughed. Was she actually warming up to these two? They were kind of fun and yes, charming. They bought her a glass of wine before heading out on their escapade to the drag queen show at Club Rendez-Vous, which turned out to be far more fun than Nikki anticipated. They all laughed hysterically when they saw that one of the drag queens on the stage bore a strong resemblance to Tara Beckenroe. Tara was the Napa Valley gossip and a staff writer for Winemaker Magazine. She had also made it her ambition in life to get into Derek's pants and pocketbook. When Nikki had first come on board at Malveaux, Tara had not so subtly explained that she had every intention of winding up as Mrs. Malveaux. She'd given Nikki strict orders to keep her distance from Derek. Nikki made a point, in return, to ignore Tara.

"She so looks like the Wicked Witch of the East!" Simon roared. "Has she been bugging you as of late, Goldilocks? I know how she likes to get under your skin."

"She does have this wild thing for Derek," Marco added, and then took a sip from his mojito, which they were drinking in abundance. Nikki was feeling no pain, but probably would in the morning. The mere mention of Tara's name usually brought on a dull headache all by itself, but tonight she was having a grand old time and not even the mention of her nemesis could ruin it.

"Does she ever," Simon replied. "What do you think of that? Scare you any?"

"No way. She's no competition."

"Ah ha!" Simon pointed at Nikki and waved a finger at her. "I knew you were in love with my brother."

"I am not."

"You are so."

She was saved as "I Will Survive," by Gloria Gaynor started playing and a large black *woman* dressed in gold lamé and fake diamonds entered and worked the room, which went wild with hoots and hollers.

After the show was over, the boys wanted to continue on, but Nikki was feeling tired and knew that she had plenty more in store for her through the weekend and needed to wake with as clear a head as possible. The boys gave her a kiss goodnight and promised to do breakfast in the a.m.

She took a cab, and a few blocks away from the hotel, had the driver let her off at Union Square so she could grab a cup of java and then walk the rest of the way, wanting some peace, fresh air, and a bit of exercise. She bought her non-fat mocha and started back to The Clift. The streets in this section were somewhat quiet and empty, as it was a weekend night and most folks were still whooping it up inside the restaurants and clubs.

She crossed the street at the corner of Geary and Taylor Street and was almost to the other side when a car tore around the block, its tires squealing against the pavement. It headed straight for her, its headlights flashed on high beam, reflecting off the darkened asphalt and nearly blinding her. The engine revved, and without any time to think, she dove to the curb as the car continued to speed down the way. A doorman from the hotel ran over to her.

"Are you all right, ma'am?" He scooped her up.

A large scrape ran down the side of her right arm, the one she dove onto, and her skirt and stockings were torn up the side. He lifted her to her feet as she nodded, but she wasn't so sure for a minute. Her body took on an almost numb-like feeling as she stared down the street where the car had raced away.

"I think so," she replied, hearing the tremor in her voice. "I'm a little tattered, but I think I'm okay. Did you see the car?"

"No. I'm sorry, I didn't. I was closing the door behind someone and all I heard was the screeching of the tires. I turned around and saw you lying there. Aren't you staying with us? I recognize you from earlier."

She nodded again.

He helped her inside the hotel. "We should really call the police," he told her.

She knew he was right, but in reality what could the police do? She didn't get a good look at the car herself. Before it tore around the corner she'd had her head down and was lost in thought. By the time she'd made the dive for the curb, she couldn't see anything in the lights. Then it was over so fast, whoever it was had taken off. It was probably some drunk who hadn't even seen her. Deep down, she wondered if that was really the case.

"No, that's okay. I'm sure the police are swamped, with it being a Friday night."

"I think we should call."

"I'll stop by the station in the morning."

The doorman finally let her go and then went over to the concierge who smiled and nodded at Nikki.

She went up to her room. Wired and now hurt, she doctored her wounds, changed into her pj's and picked up the paperback Sara Waltman had written and loaned her. She had to try and get her mind off of what just happened. She kept telling herself it was only a simple accident, and she was going to make certain she believed it. She got under her covers, and, as she was about to flip open the book, she saw that the message light on the telephone was blinking. Maybe Derek had called or maybe the boys wanted her to come back out and play some more. She

dialed the message retrieval number, and her worst fear of
the night was confirmed. The fact that someone had inten-
tionally tried to run her over became reality—a mechanical-
type voice came across the recorder, as if it had been slowed
way down like an old forty-five record, playing at thirty-
three speed. "Stop snooping. Next time you won't be so
lucky."

Chapter 17

Nikki sighed with a heaviness in her chest like she hadn't felt since she'd been fired from her acting gig and then the wait job last year. She clasped her hands together in an attempt to get them to stop shaking, the nerve system throughout her body still in overdrive. To call or not to call the police? And which police station would that be? In San Francisco, or at the sheriff's department in Santa Rosa? Because obviously this was tied into Susan Jennings' murder.

More than likely the cops here in the city would take a report and that would be about it. The sheriff and detectives in Sonoma would take it about as lightly. Everyone knew that she and Isabel were close friends, and the possibility that Nikki could be making the whole thing up would surely cross the minds of the police. The bizarre phone call could have come from a pay phone or an unavailable number, so even if the hotel had caller ID, which she doubted, it would prove fruitless. She had to face it, she was going to

wind up sounding like a paranoid bumbling idiot if she
made a police report. Or worse, a liar.

So, the next question remained, who knew she was here
in San Francisco? Well, of course there were the Boys of
Summer and even though they'd tried their damnedest to
chase her off the vineyard last year without any success,
they really did seem to have had a sincere change of heart
toward her. Maybe they were good actors, but they didn't
have a motive to kill Susan Jennings. Not one she knew
about anyway. She doubted that the boys even knew Susan.

Then there was Jennifer Jennings and her hit man Paulo.
Those two did seem like good candidates. She got out of
bed and got her purse, taking out the business card that
Paulo had given her when she'd left the condo the night before. For the first time she really looked at it. Huh? He was
a realtor like Susan. His title was in commercial sales. He
worked for one of the larger firms in the country, and Nikki
couldn't help but be surprised. She recalled him telling her
that he knew a lot about Susan. Had they worked together
and had Susan introduced him to Jennifer? Had those two
conjured up the plan to take Susan out? But how and why
set up Isabel? Because it was easy? Oh, God, Nikki's mind
was swimming in a bunch of muck trying hard to find some
answers where there didn't seem to be any.

Derek knew she was here in town. That is, if he'd
checked his messages. But he would have no reason to do
anything like this and she couldn't believe herself for even
thinking of linking his name in that second to this insanity.
And now Blake Sorgensen knew she was here. But she
hadn't told Blake or Jennifer or Paulo where she was staying, though they could have had caller ID when she'd
phoned them and saw that it came up and figured it out. Had
one of them followed her to time it just so, so they could
nearly run her over? That would have meant that whoever it

was had to have been watching from the time she and the boys left the hotel early in the evening, until she left them back at Club Rendez-Vous. That most likely being the case, then whoever it was really wanted her to leave things alone because they'd been awfully patient to tail her all night like that.

She couldn't think of anyone else who knew she was here. It was conceivable, but doubtful, that she'd been followed all the way from Sonoma. More and more, Nikki was setting her sights on Jennifer or Paulo or both, and as she rubbed the edges of Paulo's business card, she made up her mind to pay him a visit in the morning before her lunch with Sorgensen and see what he had to say about Susan. Maybe she'd get a read on him and there'd be some sign that he was involved. She'd call the mobile phone he had on his card in the morning and ask if maybe he'd be up for some coffee—somewhere very public.

For now, there was no possible way she was going to get any sleep, so she decided to pick up Sara's paperback again and started reading *Death Amongst the Vines*. Interesting title. Two hours later and halfway through the book, the story was far more interesting than just the title. The storyline was a little closer to real life than Nikki wanted to admit at that moment.

In the book the wife of the vineyard owner was murdered by drinking poisoned wine during a wedding! Granted the wife wasn't the bride, but the mother of the groom! Kristof's mother had supposedly left her family, but what if Aunt Sara had poisoned her and made her fertilizer on the back forty of the vineyard and Marty had helped to cover it up? That was paranoia talking. So, it was a similar story line, and so it was a mother who, as Nikki read on, was having an affair with a millionaire from San Francisco. The people who ran the vineyard also had a son of about seven, which from all accounts Nikki had heard, was about Kristof's age when his mom took off. Nikki was surprised that Aunt Sara had it in her to write such a risqué story or that it would have been published, but then she checked the publishing date. It was 1975; okay, so Jacqueline Susann's book *Valley of the Dolls* had already made its run along with Erica Jong's *Fear of Flying*.

Nikki couldn't put the book down until the very end, at nearly three in the morning. It was the father-in-law, or the grandpa, depending on how the reader looked at it, who had done it. This was so disturbing. Could Sara Waltman have played a part in all of this—the real thing? Could she have murdered Susan? She certainly had no problems expressing her distaste for the woman who had briefly been her great-niece by marriage. But that wouldn't have accounted for what had happened to Nikki earlier in the evening. She doubted that Sara would have had the wherewithal to follow her into the city, try to run her down, and then use some kind of crude technology to disguise her voice on the hotel's messaging system. The woman couldn't even walk without the use of a cane. If she was behind Susan's murder, then she was in cahoots with someone else. Finally, without any more desire or strength to stay awake, Nikki shut her eyes and went to sleep with thoughts of ninety-year-old grand-motherly types going on a murdering rampage.

She woke up startled and groggy as the phone on her bedside rang in her ear. At first she didn't realize that she wasn't in her own bed, and it took a second as her mind processed everything. She picked up the phone. "Hello?"

"Hello, *Bellisima*."

She plopped back down on the pillow. It was Marco. "Hi." She glanced over at the clock—seven. Four hours sleep, ugh.

"Simon doesn't ever wake before ten, and I'm one to get

up in the morning and get going, no matter what the night before might have brought on. You should have stayed with us and had some more party time. We had a wonderful time. That's a-okay. Okay? I figure since you are always so fresh faced and bright-eyed as you Americans say, that you would awaken by now. Yes, you will meet me for coffee downstairs, no?"

"Sure. Why not?" Nikki knew that as she became fully awake her mind would start off on its tangents again and that she wouldn't get back to sleep. Aunt Cara used to always remind her that the early bird catches the worm, and the worm she wanted to catch was more like a snake. She needed to get that early start because there was a lot on her agenda today, and even more after reading through Sara Waltman's book last night. "I'll see you in a half an hour."

"*Perfetto.*"

A half an hour later Nikki was scrubbed with a dab of makeup on and her shampooed hair slicked back into a ponytail. The May morning in the City of Love made her want to climb back under the down duvet upstairs in her hotel room, as the typical gloom of cloud cover hung overhead. She'd seen it through the window when she'd pulled back the drapes. It probably wouldn't burn off for quite some time, so she'd put on a white turtleneck that wouldn't only keep her warm, but also hide the scrape and bruise on her arm. She didn't need Marco asking unwanted questions. She paired the sweater with jeans and made her way to the elevator.

Marco was already seated in the restaurant, daintily pouring cream into his coffee when she walked in. She slid into the chair across from him.

"Good morning. Did you have a night of good rest?" he asked.

Before Nikki knew it, she blubbered out the whole story. Marco sat up straight. "Ah, so you are playing detective again? Your story to Derek about seeing a writing coach was a deception. Not good, *Bellisima*. But I understand your plight, and Simon and I are going to help you." He waved a finger at her.

"Excuse me?"

"Every good detective needs a partner. I watch all the television police shows and I learn this. You now have two."

"No, no. What can you do? Please, I can't let you get involved. I just needed someone to talk to. I'll take care of what I need to today and you two go tour the city. This afternoon we'll meet up for happy hour."

He shook his head. "No." He leaned in closer over the table, placing his chin in the palms of his hands. "I want you to know that Simon and I have every apology for the way we treated you when you came to Napa Valley. We were jealous and Simon wanted to be the ruler of the vineyard. The king. No more what we want. It's not. We have changed our motives and ways in the past months and that's one of the reasons we wanted to join you and treat you in the city. We need to make amends."

Nikki was taken aback by his apology. "Thank you. I appreciate that. You two *were* kind of hard on me." She laughed remembering the antics the two of them had pulled to chase her away from the winery. Everything had changed since then, like things do, so she couldn't continue to hold a grudge. "But you can't get involved in this. I don't know what's going on, but I can't let you do it."

"You want to see your friend free, don't you? And you don't think she murdered that woman, do you?"

"Yes, and no."

"Let us help."

The waiter came over and Nikki ordered a mushroom and cheese omelet along with sourdough toast and a mocha. Today was not a day for dieting, or, as all the eating healthy and exercise gurus wrote in the mass of books out on the shelves, "an eating lifestyle change." No, today was definitely not a day for an eating lifestyle change. Maybe she could use the help that Marco was proposing. There was a lot she wanted to get done today and some support would be appreciated. After last night she'd felt kind of alone in this thing. "What do you suggest?" she asked.

"Whatever you need."

Over breakfast, she finished telling Marco all of the details of what had occurred and what she'd found out since Susan's murder. Marco concocted a plan with her. She felt wary about it, and didn't know if it would work or if it was prudent, but he kept reassuring her.

"Listen to me, *Bellisima*, before I become a famous designer I have my time in the poor section of Italy, and I learned as a boy how to pick a lock and do things that I am not proud of. I steal a few things in my life, and now I am so sorry, but today my old skills they will come in handy."

"I don't know, Marco. I don't think it's safe. These people could be very dangerous; and what if you two get caught?"

He waved a hand at her, brushing off her comment. "That will not happen. You go and see this Paulo man and then this Blake slimeball."

She laughed.

"That is what you call sneaky here. No? I am only telling you how you say it to me. The man is a slimeball, you tell me."

She nodded and finished the remnants of her coffee, now fully awake and satiated. "He is."

"*Bellisima*, you don't know if any of these people are killers so you be very careful."

"You have to be more careful than I do. At least I'll be in public."

Marco looked at his watch. "I'm going to go wake my love, and we shall plan for the day. You take care of your business and we meet here at four o'clock." He stood and kissed her on the cheek, reminding her of Andrés for a second. The men of the romance countries did know how to be charming, didn't they?

Nikki took out her cell phone and prepared to call Paulo Borrelli, hoping to reach him. It was almost nine. She watched Marco head toward the elevator as her gut swam in a wave of emotion. She was still not totally convinced that it was such a good idea to allow Marco and Simon to break into what was now Jennifer Jennings' home.

Chapter 18

Paulo agreed—actually more than agreed; he sounded way too eager to make contact with Nikki, and this put her even further on guard. They met at the Starbucks just around the corner from her hotel at ten. Paulo was all Armani'd out—a bit too dapper for a Saturday morning coffee. One also had to wonder where his other half was and if she'd truly forgiven him from the night before.

They sat down at a corner table, and Nikki knew that the best defense was a good offense, so she played ball like any good quarterback and threw one right at him. "Did you and Jennifer have a chance to patch things up last night after I left?"

"Ah, that was nothing, like I told you. My little Jenny forgets that we made an agreement to have an open relationship."

Paulo reached across the table and tried to take Nikki's

hand in his, which she quickly wrapped around her coffee cup. "That's nice," she replied.

"It is. It works well and the theatrics that you saw are simply that. Theatrics. It makes things a bit more spicy for us." He winked at her and rubbed his thumb and pointer finger over his other thumb. Trying to be nonchalant about it.

Could this bozo get any sleazier?

"But there is always room for more spice."

"Speaking of, you said that you knew Susan Jennings quite well, or at least you implied that you did."

"Yes. Susan was an amazing woman in many ways."

Was that sadness in his eyes? Could this man actually have that sort of feeling? "How so?"

"She was an extremely intelligent woman, and sexy as hell." He looked away.

"I have to ask. How well did you know Susan?"

"It's none of your business, but since you asked, a lot of men knew Susan very well, but I knew her better than most. Sexy as hell, like I said—a real she-devil, that one. If anyone could have tamed her, well, baby, you're looking at him."

It was getting thick in the Starbucks, and Nikki took a drink from her coffee to keep herself from telling him what she really thought of his bravado. "That said, and assuming it means what I think it means, what happened? Why settle for the sister?"

He laughed. "You mean seconds? Yeah, well, I'm not one to settle down, but I did like Susan a lot and we had a good thing for a while. Then some older dude she thought she could get a decent payout from came along, so she started making it with him, you know. I make good money, but not like this hombre did, or used to anyway. I saw that old dude at the wedding. I guess Suzy Q liked inviting all the old flames."

"But she obviously dumped him, too."

"Oh yeah. The richer the better, and Kristof Waltman was the richest by far. Susie Q made a decent living and always lived high on the hog, but that Waltman family, well . . . You've seen their place. They make a lot of moolah, baby. I'm not surprised that someone was murdered there. I'm only surprised it was Suz."

"Really? What do you mean by that? Who would you think would've been the murder victim?"

"Sweetheart, I knew Susan really well, and she was never the type to fall in love. Men weren't her passion. Oh, yeah, she liked the old sausage of love, but money was her first love. Her real gig. If anyone was gonna get axed in that marriage, I'd have thought it would've been down the line and that it would've been the hubby. In my world I would've placed bets that the killer would've been dear Suzy Q herself."

"Interesting. Why, then, do you think Susan was murdered, and who do you think might have murdered her?"

"They got your friend behind bars don't they? Signed, sealed, and delivered, from what I heard."

Nikki couldn't help but cringe. "Yes, Isabel is in jail, but get this straight—nothing at all is signed, sealed, or delivered." She shook a finger at him.

"Hey, baby, you don't have to go getting all testy on me. I'm only going by what I hear and read." He held his hands up in the air, palms facing her, as he leaned back into his chair.

Keep cool and keep him talking. Suck it up. "I'm sorry. I don't believe that Isabel killed Susan no matter what the police or press are saying. She didn't do it."

"How do you know that? How can you be so sure? I heard the cops have some pretty solid evidence and that Suz was her nastiest self around your friend Isabel. And trust me, I have seen Susan at her *nastiest* self, and not even I would want to go toe-to-toe with that woman. There's been a time or two I wanted to take her out and teach her a lesson for being a bad girl."

"Really? Did you?"

"Hell, no. I liked screwing her too much and, like I said, I'm not a committing type of man. Even after we parted, and she hooked up with the old dude and then Waltman, every once in awhile she came to me for some real lovin'. We always had a good time together."

"And she didn't mind that you were also sharing the, uh, love sausage, with her sister?"

"Why should she? She was banging this and that and all for the dinero. She came to me for a good time. At least I was keeping it all in the family and with Jennifer it obviously isn't for the money. Well, maybe now that she has some, it makes things more fun. Just kidding."

Was he?

"Jennifer is a wild cat, and she likes to live life as a drama, just like Susan did, but with Jennifer I'm always in control. With Susan she took control, and for a man like me, that can be a bit difficult at times."

"Susan and Jennifer were obviously different, but they must've loved each other. They were sisters, after all."

"Love? Maybe a bit. You're right. They were blood sisters, and that's why I convinced Susan to include Jennifer in her will."

"You did that?"

He nodded. "But for Susan, it was more about guilt."

Nikki shifted in her chair and almost spilled her coffee on herself. "Guilty for what?"

"Those two had it rough growing up. Susan made out better than Jennifer because she was far more resilient and far more savvy. Susan left her baby sister behind."

"You've got to be more specific than that."

"Typical dysfunctional family story. They grew up poor white trash."

Nikki cringed. Those were words she'd heard before, when she'd been a little kid back in Tennessee before she'd been sent to live with her aunt. "So, their mom and dad were poor?" This was info she'd already figured out from speaking with Jennifer, but she wanted Paulo's take.

"It's more than that. Daddy left them all high and dry when the girls were real young. He was a loser, you know, the always drunk kind."

Nikki nodded. "Tough stuff."

"Yeah, the dude left them, and their mom did what she could. They lived in Arizona. Mom cleaned houses for rich folks in Scottsdale. Sometimes the girls would have to tag along, and believe me, Susan was all eyes and ears."

"She told you this?"

"Oh yeah." He nodded emphatically. "Like I told you, we were tight for a while there." He held up his hand and crossed two fingers. "As a kid, she started listening to those rich people and how they came into money and how they spent and saved, soaking up everything she could hear."

"Smart."

He pointed a finger at her, shaking it. "Told you, and sneaky. Jennifer liked the wealth, too, but like I said, savvy isn't what my girl Jenny is all about. She may like the cash, but actually that girl has a pretty big heart, and she goes way too much on emotion than anything else. All she is, is one big act. Trust me, there's a real sweet girl under there."

Okay, if he said so, but Nikki had her doubts.

"Mom wasn't as smart as her oldest daughter, and she started stealing from those she worked for."

"And she got caught."

"You're smart, too, aren't you? I like that," he replied.

"Did their mom go to jail?"

"Not only that. She served her time. The kids went to a foster home, and I guess lucky for them, depending on how you look at it, they got to stay together. Once their mom was out of jail, the dumb broad didn't even try to locate the girls. Susan has been looking over her shoulder for dear old mama to show up all these years, figuring that if she ever found her that her hand would be out like the beggar on the street."

"The girls have had no clue where their mother is or has been?"

"Nope. Surprise for Susan when Jen came knocking at her door. She wasn't too happy about that either. She tolerated her, and I think I saw a few seconds over the last year of what could be thought of as affection between them, especially when Susan was handing over a check to her sister."

"Jennifer was taking money from Susan." She said it more as a statement than question, knowing this answer, too.

"On a regular basis, but Susan was getting pretty sick of it. She had the dough and marrying into the cash flow of the century was gonna be a big help, but she didn't like feeling sucked on. She put up with it though."

"Because she felt guilty? You still haven't told me what Susan felt guilty about toward Jennifer. If anyone should feel guilty it should be their mother."

"Guilt and family is a funny thing. In the foster system the girls went from home to home. In their teen years they wound up with a fairly well-to-do family. Susan got real close with the dad, if you know what I mean. When the foster mom found out, she kicked out both of the girls, and they each split up, going out on their own. Susan wanted to come here to California and Jen wanted to stay because she'd met a guy, who, of course, knocked her up."

"Jennifer has a child?"

"She did. She went on the system, had her baby, and the baby later died of SIDS. The woman has not had it easy. She's struggled from this job to that and from this man to that. She's a looker. You've seen her."

That was true. Jennifer was pretty, but she badly needed a makeover. She seemed to have the belief that more of everything was better than less—more makeup, more cleavage. Nikki was sure that Jennifer could be far more attractive by showing off less. "Both of these women filled you in on all of this? Their life story?"

"I am *good* with the ladies." He leaned back in his chair and winked at her.

Yuck.

"I probably shouldn't be telling you any of this, but you seem like a nice lady, and who knows, maybe I'll want something from you someday."

Comment ignored. Nikki figured the guy wasn't being an open book for her because he was a nice man who liked to talk, but that didn't matter, because whatever his reasons were to be flapping his mouth the way he was didn't concern her. She pursued more questions. "Do you think Jennifer could've killed her sister?"

He laughed. "Jennifer couldn't kill a damn spider crawling across the floor the other night."

"The spider didn't have a will with Jennifer in it."

"Maybe not, but why would Jen do something like that? For the condo? No. There may have been bad blood between the girls, but they did love each other. They were sisters, and not only that, why would you want to kill the cash cow?"

"Because the cow owned a real nice condominium here in the city worth a helluva lot of money, more than, I'm sure, Susan was giving her on a regular basis."

"I see your point, but I've been investing for Jenny some of that money Susan was giving her, because I'd like to see her do well for herself. It's not in her to kill Susan, and why risk it? Why risk all that she's gained? No, sweetheart, you're barking up the wrong tree. Besides, my girl Jenny doesn't have the skills or finesse to carry out murder."

"What about you?" Why not go for it? Someone had tried to run her down the night before, and she wanted to see if she accused this man, if he wouldn't squirm. She wanted some answers and fast. She knew Isabel's time was running out and the thought of her sitting in that jail cell in Santa Rosa was heartbreaking.

"Not only are you smart"—he clucked his tongue—"but you're a goddamn comedian, too. Why would I want to kill the best lay I've had in my entire life? Trust me, Susan would've been back in my bed in no time, once the honeymoon was over, regardless of her marriage vows."

"And, it didn't bother you that you were sleeping with both Susan and Jennifer, and it really didn't bother Susan?"

He shrugged. "It's sex, babe. Total ecstasy. Who gives a shit? Jennifer might have cared if she knew what was going on, but she never knew and she never had nor has a need to know. Especially now." He stared pointedly at her.

She got his drift. Nikki wondered silently if Jennifer did know that she was sharing a bed with her very own sister and if her motive to kill wasn't about money at all, but over a man. This was getting a bit too Jerry Springer for her.

"I may have the finesse and brains to murder someone, but I don't have a need. Why bother? I have everything I could ever want and desire, and I don't have a problem getting the things I don't have. Killing people is not how I get what I want. Besides what could be my motive? I have my own money, which I do very well at earning, and I don't take handouts. Never been my style, so killing for Susan's money wouldn't be up my alley, and if it was, and I know what you're thinking . . . If it was about money, and since I put Susan up to including Jenny in her will, you're thinking maybe I got greedy. I hook up with Jenny and get my own piece of the pie."

"You said it, not me."

"If that was my deal, I sure in hell would've waited until she was married to Waltman for a bit, and convince Jenny to cozy up to big sis a little more. Have her get in good and tight and then kill Susan. I'd wind up with more myself. Besides I'd have married Jenny first to make sure I got what I thought was mine. But, sorry, sweetheart, that wasn't or isn't my deal. Murder is not my style."

Surprisingly enough, Nikki believed him. The man was an egomaniac, but a murderer? She had her doubts. However, she still wasn't convinced that Jennifer hadn't done away with her own sister. Nikki had to wonder if it was possible that Jennifer did indeed know she was sharing her bed buddy with her own flesh and blood. Could Jennifer have gotten rid of Susan over a man? Even if it was this creep? She didn't think Jennifer was as dumb as Paulo did. He might be underestimating his girlfriend or whatever she was to him, but Nikki wasn't about to.

"I know you want to help your friend out and I can get that. Sad thing is, I think you might have to face it. Your friend, in all likelihood, murdered Susan. I heard a rumor going around that your friend Isabel and Kristof had a thing at one time."

Nikki had to bite her tongue. How dare he. He didn't know Isabel. "Where did you hear something like that?"

"I have my ways. Listen, it's been great speaking with you, and I do hope I cleared up some things for you. I told you what I did in confidence, because some people may have the wrong idea about Susan and Jenny. They're both decent women who had rough starts in life. Susan wasn't always the nicest person around, but she didn't deserve to die. And, if you want my opinion, Jenny is an innocent by-stander who is finally going to maybe get a chance to enjoy life a little. Granted it's at the expense of her sister, but life is bizarre that way." He stood and took her hand, giving it another one of his slimy kisses. "If I can ever help you out in *any* way, you know how to find me."

Paulo left and Nikki went into the bathroom to wash her hands. Maybe Paulo hadn't done it, but he'd told a huge tale and Nikki wondered why. Had he really thought that she might wind up in the sack with him after spilling all he knew about the Jennings women? Or had he had ulterior motives to either deflect suspicion off of him and onto Jennifer? Or was his need to tell all about trying to convince Nikki that Jennifer was just an all-American girl under-neath that tough exterior?

Nikki had no idea. She really didn't think he'd murdered Susan, but maybe Jennifer had, and he knew it. Maybe he was trying to protect Jennifer.

She checked her watch. Time was racing by and she only had an hour before her lunch with Blake Sorgensen. So maybe she hadn't just had coffee with a murderer, but she couldn't help wondering if she was about to have lunch with one, because the photos she'd seen at the Waltman Castle might have been Blake Sorgensen's reason for killing Susan.

Chapter 19

Blake Sorgensen suggested they meet at The Boulevard, which was across from the ferry landing and had beautiful views of the Bay Bridge and amazing artwork, including a mosaic of a peacock that covered the bar room floor. Such a shame Nikki had to waste the amazing view and eclectic beauty from inside the restaurant with puffed-up, puffed-out Blake Sorgensen.

"A bit surprised to have you call me, Miss Sands. At first I wasn't sure who you were, but then I remembered that you were the lovely young woman I met the other day at the wedding." He hung his head for a few seconds. Then looked back up and out at the ocean. He reached for the scotch and soda he'd ordered.

Nikki thought his eyes were glassed over from more than just the booze. "I tried reaching you for a few days, like I explained over the phone. I'm glad I finally reached you."

.

"I told you before that I've given up on young women."
He laughed. It was sad laughter. "Besides, Gorgeous, aren't
you and that fine young man you were with on Saturday an
item?"

"No. Actually, he's my boss."

"Right. I've heard that said before. One of my girl-
friends used to say that, too." He leaned across the table
and whispered, "What? Is he married?"

"God, no. He really is my boss." Nikki quickly scanned
the menu and ordered a chicken salad.

"Whatever, dear." He lit one of his stogies.

She shifted in her chair away from the smoke. "I called
because of Susan's murder."

He swirled the contents of his drink. "I'm stunned and
deeply saddened. I had no idea of the situation, until your
phone call. As I believe you were aware, I left the reception
early to catch a flight out of town. I'm at a loss as to why
you phoned me and insisted we meet. I can't see what I
could possibly say or do."

"Oh. I think that maybe you do. I was a friend of Susan's." Nikki was getting way too good at these little white
lies. "I'm also a friend of the woman the police have arrested, and I know she couldn't have done such a horren-
dous thing. I need to know what your relationship was with
Susan."

He leaned in again, scotch and tobacco on his breath.
"Don't bullshit an old bullshitter, honey. Cut to the chase. I
know you weren't dear old friends with Susan. You're also
certainly not a detective. Bottom line, what do you want
from me? For some reason, I suspect that you already
know what the nature of my relationship with Susan was."

"You're right. Let's cut to the chase."

The waiter set down Nikki's salad and Diet Coke. She

picked through the salad with her fork for a minute, wanting Blake to squirm. He didn't appear to be much of a squirmer until she looked back up to him and said, "Did Susan break that old bullshitter heart of yours? Did you take your hurt and anger out on her by killing her?" Ooh, boy, she was getting either brave or stupid at this game.

His bloodshot eyes snapped to attention. "Where do you get off?"

Nikki set down her fork. Blake picked up his drink. His idea of lunch was apparently that of the liquid kind.

"I get off saying this because my best friend is sitting in a jail cell in Santa Rosa for a crime I know she didn't commit. I also know because you admitted it to me that you were conveniently out of town for the past few days, and since you know that I know you and Susan were more than friends, I have to wonder if you may have been involved with putting your lover six feet under, and then you ran away to Mexico to wait for things to cool off."

Blake Sorgensen slammed back the rest of his drink and waved to the waiter, and then pointed to his glass. "Think I'll need another one for this conversation." His eyes brimmed with tears.

"You might." This moment would probably be a good time to change her tactic. The man was half looped and now emotional. Being sympathetic might draw more of the truth from him than going the hard-nosed route. She touched his gnarled hand. "I'm sure the police may find out about your relationship."

"I hope not. I don't want Kristof or Marty to know. I would never want to hurt Kristof like that. Can I ask you how you knew?"

"Woman's intuition." She didn't know if now was the time to spring it on him that there were some photo stills hanging around that might put Paris Hilton to shame. Nikki also didn't want to break it to him that Kristof may have already known, and probably Marty, too. "I can completely understand that you wouldn't want them to know, since you're such a good and dear old friend. You and Susan had quite a thing, I take it."

"I loved her. I really loved her. Hell, I'm such a fool. I'm the one who introduced her to Kristof. He had no idea about us, and at first I didn't know the two of them were seeing each other." The waiter set down the refill on the scotch.

"You introduced them?" Those psych and self-help books she read on occasion had something to them, because he was blabbering. "I make most of my real estate deals up on the northern coastline in Mendocino or Monterey. I live in Mendocino most of the time, but I keep a place here in the city because I like to change it up once in a blue moon. Marty came to me and said that Kristof was looking for a place in the city, that he liked to visit here a lot on the weekends and wanted to have an apartment out this way. Susan dealt mainly with real estate in the city so I connected the two of them. They obviously hit it off."

"When did she tell you about them?"

"Not too long after they started dating. You know what she said?"

Nikki shook her head.

"She told me that she loved me. That she adored me. However, she wanted children and so did Kristof. How could I deny her that? She knew I wasn't going to ever have children with her. What could I do? I did the right thing and let her go."

"But you still saw her didn't you?"

He nodded. "We did still see each other on occasion. I loved her. I needed her. I begged her to see me."

"When was the last time?"

"Two weeks ago. At my beach house. I pleaded with her to change her mind about marrying Kristof. I even told her that maybe we could have children. I could have a reversal on my vasectomy. But she told me no, and that she couldn't see me anymore. She knew I was coming to the wedding, and she said that after the wedding she never wanted to see me again."

"Can I ask you, if you gave her money when she visited you?"

Blake looked away and then back at her. "I'm a sorry sack. I did." His tears were now streaming down his face. "I would've done anything for her, but the one thing I couldn't give her was what she wanted and now she's gone. I still can't believe she's gone." He wiped his face and then brought his napkin to his nose and blew hard.

What was it with Susan that the men she took advantage of stayed stuck to her like a fly on a sticky strip? She hadn't been the sweetest gal in the world, but then again, Paulo and Blake weren't exactly top-notch. Sure, they had some cash and Susan liked cash, but class? Not a lot of that. Blake had to have seen through her. One would've thought of midlife crises with him, but the way he was carrying on, maybe he'd really loved her. She was gorgeous, even from a woman's perspective. Were the men Susan sunk her nails into so shallow that what was beneath Susan's skin didn't matter to them? Apparently so. Nikki took a few more bites of her lunch, which was delicious, but it wasn't settling well. None of this was settling well.

Waiting for the bill, Blake finished his drink. For a moment he appeared to sober up as he said, "I want to make this clear to you, and I will tell the police if they ask, I loved Susan. I loved her wholeheartedly, enough to let her go and make a life for herself, have a family. I wanted the best for her. I really loved that woman. I would've never killed her.

Never. I'm sorry that your friend is in jail, but your insinuation that I may have killed Susan is very wrong." With that statement he polished off his drink.

"That said, do you have any idea who would've killed her? Who might have wanted her dead?"

He set his napkin on top of his plate and stood. "I have no idea. This hasn't been the pleasant lunch I'd hoped for and I simply need to go home and rest." He turned and walked out of the restaurant, leaving the bill for Nikki to pay.

A thought came to Nikki as she looked out the window at the bridge and bay, concerning Blake Sorgensen's emphatic denial of killing his beloved Susan. Who was the man trying to convince? Nikki or himself? Because as far as Nikki was concerned, Blake had had a good reason to want to murder Susan. It was called that thin line between love and hate. Had Blake Sorgensen crossed it when Susan hadn't made her way back into his arms?

Chapter 20

Nikki decided to make one last stop before heading back to the hotel. She doubted she'd get anywhere with where she was going because private investigators weren't exactly known to give out information. But she had to give it a try and see if she couldn't find out who had hired the private investigative team of Lawson and Rennert, the guys who'd taken the X-rated photos of Blake and Susan. If Blake wasn't the killer, which Nikki was not ruling out, then maybe whoever had them followed was. The envelope had been addressed to Sara Waltman, and after reading through Sara's sordid mystery, she didn't discount the old woman as a suspect either.

Nikki had memorized the address for the offices of the private investigative team. It was on California Street. But when Nikki arrived there, what stood in its place was none other than a pizzeria. Maybe she'd memorized the address incorrectly. She dialed information on her cell, and, to her surprise, discovered that there was no Lawson and Rennert in the San Francisco or surrounding areas. Why the bogus address? Nikki had no clue and no time to investigate further. She had to meet the boys back at the hotel.

By the time Nikki made it back to The Clift, it was almost four o' clock and she was dog tired. Had she just had lunch with a murderer? But could he have remained sober long enough to do the deed? Or had she had coffee with one that morning, or a drink the night before with a lunatic sibling, and who in the hell had given the bogus address and sent those photos of Blake and Susan? She didn't know. What she did know was that she was more confused than before starting out that morning. Less than twenty-four hours ago someone had made a desperate attempt to steer her clear from discovering the truth, and that someone was still out there. Who knew if they'd make another attempt, because she certainly hadn't backed off, like they'd insisted she do. She'd plowed right ahead, more resolute than ever to seek justice for Isabel.

She plopped down on one of the lobby sofas and took a quick glance around to see if she noticed anyone suspicious keeping tabs on her.

Nothing but a family with two kids registering at the front desk—hardly the first thing to come to mind as being questionable. However, watching them did make her think. There was a little girl and boy, twins, actually, of about three, and they were having a good time playing patty-cake with one another. Nikki's heart started doing that thing it had just recently started doing when she got around children. Even after the bizarre, exhausting day she couldn't help but smile at the toddlers whose joyful faces sent a bittersweet pang through her. A family would be nice. The mom and dad looked tired but happy. The husband finished the paperwork and gave his wife a kiss. Then he picked up the little girl, and swung his arm over his wife's shoulder. Their little boy held onto his mom's hand. Maybe someday.

It was now after four and Nikki fidgeted with her watch. Where were the boys? Marco had insisted on four o'clock. What if they'd been caught by Jennifer or Paulo, and the police were called? Or worse? Nikki couldn't allow herself to even go there. The boys had really grown on her throughout the weekend and she didn't want to consider that something might have happened to them, and that she would've been the catalyst that put them in harm's way.

She called in to check her messages, both at home and work and then on her cell. Only one message—a client ordering more wine. Not the boys. And not Derek. So much for thinking that he might actually take her up on her invite to the city so she could explain her whereabouts the other night. It was for the best. She knew she needed to put the major crush—and that's all it was—she had on Derek behind her and move on.

She started to dial Marco's cell phone number when he and Simon came bounding through the lobby doors arm in arm, smiling like two Cheshire cats and way too cheerful looking. She sighed, relieved that they were absolutely fine, but she grew pretty angry as they came closer, the reek of alcohol surrounding them.

"Sorry we're late, Goldilocks, but we've been down at the Buena Vista Café having Irish coffees. We really should've had her meet us there." Simon turned and looked at Marco, who nodded dumbly at him, his eyes glassy.

"You two have been out drinking? Do you have any idea how worried I was getting? I thought that maybe something terrible happened." She lowered her voice. "That maybe you had been caught inside that apartment by either Paulo or Jennifer."

Marco laid a hand on her shoulder, which she shrugged off. "Isn't that sweet? She loves us."

"You two didn't even go there. Did you? I knew I shouldn't have told you what was going on. I didn't want you to get involved in the first place, but then blah, blah, blah, Marco. You go and tell me, oh no, we'll help you." She put on a fake Italian accent and waved her arms about. "I'm a big pickpocket, trust me. We will help you, *Bellisima*. What a bunch of . . ."

Simon clamped his hand over her mouth. She rocked back in surprise. "Would you shut up, Goldilocks? Of course we went there, and we have something to show you. Now come on. We're going to the bar first and we'll show you what we found."

"Uh, uh. You two are already three sheets to the wind. Tell me now."

"You are being, what you call her, a spoilsport." Marco jutted his hip to the side and put a hand on it. "We no gonna tell you, if you don't come have a drink with us, and trust me, this you wanna know."

"You two are terrible, did you know that?"

Simon smiled. "When we're good, we're good, but when we're bad, well, honey . . ." He licked the tip of his finger and stuck it on his hip and made a hissing sound. "We're hot."

"Fine. It's your head and your livers you'll have to cope with."

They went inside the hotel bar and sat down at a row of open bar stools. Simon pulled a package out of his leather pack. "A round of mojitos," he sang out to the bartender, who nodded their way. Simon then opened up the package and took out a pile of photos and spread them on the table. "Somebody has been watching somebody or somebodies, should I say."

Nikki's mouth dropped. There was a whole row of photos, all of them containing pictures of Kristof and Isabel. There were photos with the two of them kissing on a yacht, the one Nikki knew the Waltmans owned. Nikki knew the Waltmans berthed up in Mendocino. Isabel had mentioned spending a weekend there with Kristof. Then there were photos of them holding hands in the parking lot at Grapes, photos of them hugging, and even a picture which someone had taken outside Isabel's window while the two of them were kind of looking like they were getting ready to do the naked tango. Nikki had seen enough, too much in fact, of her friend and Kristof.

"Where did you find these?" she asked.

"Actually, we pretty much tore that place apart," Simon said. "At first, I didn't know if it was a good idea. I mean, we were breaking the law for you, Goldilocks, but Marco insisted that you have nothing but good intentions and that helping you out would be a good way for making up to you all the bad things we kinda said and did a while back. We are sorry, you know."

"I know, I know. Okay, already. Where did you find the pictures?"

"Good intentions or not, that doesn't sound very grateful." Simon frowned at her.

"I'm sorry. It's been a long hard day and all I want to do is find out who murdered Susan Jennings so that Isabel can get out of jail and live her life."

"Long hard day? Don't we know. We're like criminals today, which by the way totally goes against our ethics these days, you know especially after studying under Guru Sansibaba. He says that the journey to enlightenment forces us to leave behind all criminal activity, be it from the smallest of lies, to wherever the greedy heart takes us in achieving only the material."

"It's for the higher good," Marco interrupted. "Guru Sansibaba also says that truth for the higher good is all important in releasing us from the material. We must remember that an innocent woman is in jail. Right, Bellisima?"

"I'm going to wring both of your necks and then fly out to Sedona and wring Guru Sansibaba's neck if you don't tell me where you found these photos!"

"We found the pictures inside a book in the dining room."

"How did you know to look there?" she asked.

"We didn't. It was inside Dante's *Inferno,* which I absolutely adore," Simon replied. "I decided to take it off the shelf and flip through it. Out dropped the pictures and we knew they meant something. I know what Kristof Waltman looks like and I've seen Isabel around. We also went to opening night at Grapes. Remember that night?" He lovingly looked at Marco who smiled. "I knew it was the two of them and I thought that they might mean something. What do you think?"

"I think they definitely mean something. Susan knew that Kristof and Isabel were having an affair and if you look at the date on these photos they were taken four months before the wedding, which was about the time Susan came to see Isabel about catering the reception. I had heard that originally she planned to have Domaine Chandon do it, but had a falling-out with the chef and claimed she wanted to give Grapes some recognition because she'd tried Isabel's cooking and loved it."

"Why marry a cheat, then?" Marco asked. "If Susan knew that Kristof was sleeping with Isabel, why not break it off with him?"

That was a good question because from what Paulo had told her earlier, Susan had no problems getting wealthy men on the line, and there were even bigger fishes in the sea than Kristof Waltman. He was a big one, but Nikki was certain

Susan could've caught something even bigger. Could Susan have really loved Kristof? "I don't know. I know these pictures mean something. What they mean, I haven't the faintest idea, other than that Susan had some proof that Kristof had cheated on her with Isabel four months before their wedding. What it doesn't tell us is who killed Susan and why."

"Listen, Goldilocks, I hate to mention this, but Marco and I have discussed a possibility that I think you may have to consider in light of these photos."

There was a long pause between the three of them as Nikki took a drink from her mojito. Simon looked away from her.

"Okay, speak, Inspector Clouseau," she said after setting down her drink.

"*Bellisima*. I think what Simon is wanting to say to you is that does the photographs of Isabel and Kristof not bring up the possibility that Isabel did commit this crime?"

"What? No! Absolutely not."

"Shouldn't you maybe consider it?" Simon asked. "Guru Sansibaba says that your reality may not be that of others, and our need for approval and love can lead us astray from our reality. Could your friendship with Isabel be clouded because of your love for her? Therefore, your reality is not the reality that is real."

"What? You two don't make any sense. Isabel is not guilty." She grabbed the photos and stood to leave. "I'll prove it, and I'll do it on my own, thank you."

"Now, *Bellisima*. Guru Sansibaba says that you should never leave a situation in anger."

"Oh for Heaven's sakes, screw Guru Sansibaba. He's just some shyster who worked you two over for a bunch of cash and fed you a bunch of bull."

Simon held up a finger. "Maybe this is true, but you must admit that you like us far better now, and we love you and know that you'll reconcile with your anger. We are only here to help."

Marco nodded emphatically. "He is right."

"You love me because you're drunk."

"No, no. We do love you and want to help."

Nikki couldn't help but laugh. Simon patted her chair seat and she reluctantly sat back down. They had helped her out today and they did know how to make her laugh.

Simon turned his head and seemed distracted. "It looks like we're not the only ones who want to come to your rescue." He scraped up the photos and shoved them into Nikki's purse. "For now, looks like we better stop playing *Charlie's Angels*, because Prince Charming is at this very moment gallivanting through the door."

Nikki followed Simon's gaze until her eyes met Derek's as he walked toward her.

Chapter 21

"Hi," Nikki said as Derek slipped into a chair next to her.

Marco smiled slyly at him, which Nikki caught. Derek actually turned red in the face, and Nikki's stomach did one of those swan dives only Olympic divers were meant to do.

Simon quickly ordered his brother a drink. Nikki overheard him say to Marco, "Get some alcohol in him, loosen him up."

"It is such a shame we can't get him to Guru Sansibaba. He could let go of all of those intimacy issues the past has created for him."

Nikki turned and glared at them.

"Don't you two have plans or something? This is *your* town," Derek said.

"Sure, sure, sure. Of course we do," Simon replied. "Maybe we could all get together later for dessert or a drink or something fun like that. I'll have my cell on."

He winked at Nikki, who wanted to deck him.

Marco leaned in and gave her a kiss on the cheek. "You be careful, *Bellisima*."

She wasn't certain if he meant be careful of getting her heart trampled on, be careful of having too good of a time, or be careful of the bad guy or guys out there who wanted her to stop playing amateur sleuth.

The boys teeter-tottered away and an awkward silence ensued between Nikki and Derek.

"You decided to come," she said.

"I did. I, uh, actually have some accounts here that could use some attention."

"I could've handled that for you." She shrank back a bit.

"I know. I thought personal attention from me was needed."

He'd come here for business and not at her behest. This man caused her nothing but confusion and, to be honest, it was getting tiring. "Right."

"Don't get me wrong. I'm sorry, Nikki. I also, I mean I really came up here to talk to you. The business is a side thing. A good excuse to take off for the weekend."

Good excuse. Well, excuse me.

"I felt bad about the other night. I was rude."

"It's not a big deal. I do wish you would've let me explain."

He shook his head. "There's no need. It's none of my business why you canceled dinner and what you did with your time."

"Maybe not, but I think you thought I was out with Andrés, and I wasn't."

She could tell he wanted to ask her more by the way he shifted on his bar stool and casually sipped his drink, one eye trained on her.

"I was out with Deirdre Dupree. I'd run into her earlier

that day in Sonoma Square. She was distressed over Susan Jennings's murder. She once had a thing for Kristof, and so I suggested we meet for dinner. At the moment I was caught up in her drama and I wasn't thinking about the fact that we already had plans. I'm sorry about that."

He set down the mojito. "I would've understood that."

"You didn't give me a chance to explain."

"I guess I didn't. Can I ask you, if you were with Deirdre, how is it that you came home with Andrés?"

Cough it up. It was shameful to her to have to tell Derek this. "Honestly, I drank too much over dinner, and he called me while I was at dinner. I knew that getting a cab that late over in Sonoma might be difficult. I told him my predicament and he came to get me."

"You could've called me. I would've come."

"I was embarrassed. You're my boss. I didn't want to bother you so late. Besides, I thought maybe you'd be miffed at me for canceling dinner, especially since it was supposed to originally be a business dinner, and then going out with Deirdre."

He laughed. "Nikki, what kind of guy do you think I am? I'm not an ass. We've all had too much to drink when we shouldn't have. At least you had the smarts to get a ride. I only wish you'd called me. Boss or not, I'm also your friend and I would've understood. But I'm glad that you and Andrés are such good friends, that you were able to turn to him." He took another sip of his drink. After setting it down he asked, "So are you two seeing each other, you know, dating?"

"No. We're not dating. I told you that the other night, and it still stands. We are *not* dating. I am spending more time with him lately because of Isabel's situation. He needs a friend right now."

"You don't think she did it, do you?"

"No way. I know Isabel. She's got a good heart and wouldn't hurt anyone."

"Are you snooping around in all of this, Nikki? Is that the reason for your dinner with Deirdre? I never knew you two were close. Not to mention, what about your sudden trip here? Is there some *lead* you're following?"

"Do you *really* want to know?"

"Yes, I do. At least, I think do."

"Fine. I'll tell you, but over dinner. My treat. That's what we agreed to, and since I already *explained* myself about the other night and I was supposed to do that over dinner, I think I still owe you dinner. Besides, didn't you tell me that there was something you wanted to discuss with me?"

He hesitated for a moment. "Yes, there is."

"Shouldn't I change?" she asked. She was still wearing the turtleneck and jeans from early that morning.

"You look great."

After so many hours and a rough day, she doubted it, but what the hell? The way he said it to her, Nikki couldn't help but believe him. Besides there was the plus that he couldn't see the bad scrape on her arm. If he did, she knew that he'd have questions and she also knew that he wouldn't like the answers.

They headed out the lobby doors and caught a cab. With Derek at her side Nikki wasn't looking over her shoulder like she had been earlier. But, she refused to entertain the thought that Isabel could truly be the killer as Simon and Marco had suggested. Still, the suggestion did nag at her, as well as the idea that maybe someone *was* still watching her.

Chapter 22

Derek and Nikki wound up at Antoine's down near the embarcadero. At first Nikki didn't make the connection, she was just happy to be with Derek, and didn't pay too much attention to the restaurant and the surroundings, other than it was old-world Italian and candlelit. She opened the menu and then the realization hit her.

"Antoine's?"

"Yes, the one you made such a nice fat sale to the other day. I'm really pleased that you got the account back for us. Right before Antoine passed away he cut off his business with us."

"Why?" she asked.

"We weren't the only ones. Antoine was having some serious money troubles, and at first he tried cutting back on his more expensive vendors, then his wait staff. He even sold off his restaurant in Chicago, hoping it would give him the cash to jump-start the rest of the restaurants."

"But it didn't?"

"No. Because he'd cut back on the better vendors and rumor travels fast in this industry. His business started to suffer."

"Is that why he had to sell off his business to Daveed and Roman?"

Derek nodded. A waiter appeared and he ordered a very nice bottle of Meritage.

"You were aware that Pamela Leiland, Susan's maid of honor, was married to Antoine, weren't you?" Nikki asked, perusing the menu and finally settling on the brie Toscano with sun-dried tomato pesto for the appetizer.

"I knew that. I'd met her once when we were still doing business with Antoine. She seemed like a nice lady. Sure, there was a lot of speculation about the age difference and everything, but I have to tell you that I really think those two were in love."

"You think so?" Nikki figured that Pamela was probably as shallow as Susan. Didn't birds of a feather flock together?

"It may not have started out that way. Who knows? Antoine was a good man, very generous, almost too generous with his kids and everyone else. It's no wonder he wound up having financial troubles. I figure it's probably what killed him in the end."

"That's a shame."

"It is. He was the kind of man who cared about the people he dealt with. He felt terrible having to sever ties with us, but he claimed that he needed to start saving cash rather than spending it. That he and Pamela were trying to have a baby and he wanted to make sure the kid had all the advantages his older kids had."

"That obviously never happened."

"No, it didn't. I'd bet he was probably a great dad."

"Did you meet his kids?" Nikki asked.

The waiter came to the table and opened the Meritage, which, after smelling and tasting it, Derek approved. The red wine with both tobacco and black cherry notes complemented the brie nicely.

"I actually met them the weekend I came to try to save the account with Antoine. They live here in the city, too, if I remember right. Nice people. Their mother died when they were little. Antoine hadn't remarried until he met Pamela."

"And they liked her?"

"It really did seem like one big happy family."

"Did the kids work in the restaurant business?"

"No. I think they did for some time, but they'd each gone their own ways. The son was involved in theater. The daughter, if I remember right, went to work with her husband in his family business."

"What was that?"

But before Derek got to answer her question, an over-the-top Daveed dressed in a white silk outfit rushed to their table. "I thought that was you, you devil, you." Daveed pointed at Derek.

Derek shook Daveed's hand. He picked up the bottle of wine Derek had ordered and called over the waiter, and handing him the wine bottle, whispered something in his ear. Daveed pulled up a chair next to them. "And you, aren't you the one who tapped us out the other day?"

Nikki mustered a smile for the obnoxious man. Not easy to do. He'd single-handedly pretty much just rained on her parade of candlelight and romance with Derek. Or at least there was the hope of romance. Not anymore.

"She is good, my friend, really good. No wonder you sent her my way. If Angel hadn't been hanging with me that day, well, this one here, she's a sweetheart. You two are obviously hanging together. You are the bomb, G."

There was nothing more annoying than a middle-aged man trying to recapture his glory days by acting like inner-city youth gone bad.

"Hey, look, here comes my sweet thang, now."

Nikki and Derek turned to see Angel, strutting over on four-inch heels, a shirt that just covered her boobs and a pair of hip-hugger white pants that didn't leave much to the imagination. Her blond hair was down around her face, and the makeup was done up sixties style, complete with shell-pink lipstick and false eyelashes.

Angel sauntered up to Daveed and planted a kiss on his cheek. She pointedly looked at Nikki and smugly smiled at her. Did she really think that Nikki cared that she was sleeping with the Hugh Hefner wannabe?

"Gang, dinner is on me. I am so excited and totally thrilled that you came in. We've done some posh things with the menu since taking over the place. I brought in Luis de Carlino from New York. He puts the old Antoine's to shame." Daveed looked skyward. "Hope he didn't hear that. He was a decent dude."

Derek looked at Nikki. "You don't need to buy us dinner, Daveed," he said.

"Of course I do. I want to. You can give me a cut on my next wine order." He winked at Nikki.

"You sell wine?" Angel asked.

Instead of going into it and reminding Miss Angel that she'd actually been to the Malveaux Winery, tasting wines and being served by Nikki less than a week ago, she simply replied, "Yes." She was getting the picture that these two weren't going to take off nicely and crawl back under the rocks they'd come out from.

The waiter brought back a bottle of Dom Perignon. "No, no. We're good with our wine," Derek said.

"I insist. Your lady here was so killer to us the other day and I want to repay her. It's all good. I love being able to talk shop with like-minded individuals."

Yeah, cause he wasn't talking shop, religion, politics, or even Cartoon Network with the booty call.

"When was she nice to you?" Angel asked.

Derek rolled his eyes at Nikki, who stifled herself to keep from laughing out loud.

"You're so sweet," Daveed said to Angel.

Nikki didn't know if she could eat anything. However, the night went on in that manner and by the time the evening came to a close, Nikki and Derek consumed quite a few bottles of wine with their host and hostess, ate more than a small country might, and tried to contain themselves from cracking up at the stupid remarks Angel and Daveed made often.

Walking out the front door and across the street to catch a cab, they finally let go with some bellyaching laughter. The combination of too much wine and the relief of being out of the restaurant caused the shared laughter to go on for several minutes.

Nikki finally caught her breath. She rubbed Derek's arm. "I don't get it. How can a nine by thirteen pan, be the same as a thirteen by nine pan," she said, mocking Angel from a conversation that had occurred over dinner, when the young woman tried to explain her attempt at making brownies yesterday for her *lover*. "I had to throw it all away, because the pan I had was a thirteen by nine inch, and I couldn't, like, lick the bowl because I'm a vegetarian." Nikki batted her eyelashes and fell against Derek. They both started laughing again.

"Poor kid. She pretty much takes the cake for dumb blondes," he said.

"I wouldn't have believed it, if I hadn't see it and heard it with my own eyes, and believe me, I've seen a lot of dumb people in my day."

Derek opened the door to the cab and they slipped in the back seat. They sat very close together—touching. Nikki wanted to put her head on his shoulder and close her eyes, never leave this cab. He faced her and grew serious. "I'm sorry they interrupted our dinner and time together."

"No apology necessary. It was free entertainment."

"You still have that great sense of humor. I love that about you."

"Thanks."

"I wanted to talk to you tonight a bit more about you and your snooping into this murder investigation," Derek said.

"I have to prove that Isabel didn't kill Susan."

"I know." He patted her knee. "But shouldn't the police be doing that?"

"How could they? They've stopped investigating. They believe that the killer is behind bars and I can't stand by and let my friend, whom I know is innocent, take the fall."

He nodded. "I'm worried about you. It's dangerous, what you're doing. I believe that Isabel is innocent, too, but you're putting yourself out there and whoever the killer is could come after you. I could probably pull some strings over at the station and see if somehow they will reopen the case."

"You know they won't. I'm being careful. Trust me." The phantom stalker from the night before came to mind, but she wasn't about to mention it to him. "I have to do this for her. Tell me that you understand. It's not going to inter- fere with my work and I promise I'll be careful." She faced him and smiled. "I didn't know you cared so much."

"Of course I care. I do understand."

It grew quiet inside the cab. Nikki didn't say anything un- til she looked up and saw that the cab driver was watching them in the rearview mirror. He, too, was apparently waiting to see what would happen next. "I know that you had a purpose for our dinner. What was it?"

He shook his head. "You know what, you're not going to get off that easy. Daveed bought our dinner tonight. I'm thinking you still owe me."

"You do, do you?"

"I do. I also figure, it's a good way for me to get to have another dinner with you."

There he was, flirting with her again. "You're not going to tell me what you wanted to talk about tonight, until I take you to dinner again?"

"Nope. But I'm actually going to take you out. Then you will still owe me, and I'm guaranteed a third dinner with you."

"Won't people start to talk?"

"Let them." He leaned in, and Nikki knew this was it. He was going to kiss her. She closed her eyes, and then nearly went through the windshield as the cabbie slammed on his brakes and started yelling obscenities. Nikki's eyes popped open to see a half-naked Marco running across the street, drunk and crazed. He was wearing some type of white balloon looking pants and no shirt—a surreal, gay *I Dream of Jeannie*. Nikki had to blink her eyes several times to make certain she was really seeing what she thought she was.

Derek flew out of the car. They were in front of their hotel. "What the hell is going on?" He grabbed Marco by the shoulder.

"Derek! Oh no, it is terrible. I'm so glad you're here. I tried to call you on your cellular phone, but couldn't reach you."

"What's the problem, Marco?"

Nikki stepped out of the cab.

"It's Simon. We were down at Club Townsend having a

beautiful evening, when a young man started to talk with me. I didn't do a thing. I would never betray Simon. I love him." He sobbed and threw his bare arms in the air.

"Marco, what happened?"

"I tried to get Simon to stop. I had thoughts that after all of our Zen meditation, and the studying of and with Guru Sansibaba, that he would have been rid of his temper and jealousy. I am afraid that he is not. He hit the poor boy and started a fight at the club. He is downtown in the jail. Can you get him out, please?"

"Me? Why me? Why can't you?"

"During the fight, my wallet was stolen from me."

Nikki walked over next to Derek. "We should help them."

Derek sighed and agreed. "You don't need to. I'll take care of it. You go in and get some sleep."

"No. I'll go with you."

"Trust me, Nikki, it might be a long night. I'd feel better if you went up to your room and rested. I'll deal with this mess. You've been wonderful all night to put up with Daveed and what's her name. I certainly don't expect you to come down to the holding tank now. Please go on up." He kissed her cheek. "We'll have dinner next week. I promise it won't turn out like this."

She smiled at him and watched as he handed Marco his jacket, insisting he put it on. They then got inside the cab she'd just been in with Derek and rode away.

Chapter 23

For the second time that weekend, Nikki woke to the phone ringing. When she lifted it, she was relieved to hear Derek's voice on the other end.

"Hey, you. I'm so sorry about last night."

She stretched and sat up straight under the down comforter. "No worries. How did it go?"

"Fine. They released him after I posted bail. I'm sure he has a nasty hangover today, and a black eye to boot."

"Oh, God. You're kidding? Well, at least he has Marco to take care of him."

"He almost didn't. Marco was pretty angry with Simon last night. Besides getting my brother out of jail, I also had to play relationship counselor to the two of them. I finally got Marco to mellow out. I'm sure they're nursing their wounds back at the hotel right now."

"What? Aren't you still here?" she asked. She figured he'd also still be at the hotel this morning.

"Don't I wish. That's why I'm calling. I really wanted to give you a ride back to Napa today, but about the time I got back to sleep this morning I got a phone call from Manuel." Derek referred to the vineyard manager.

"I hear an edge in your voice. What's up?"

"Besides being up all night and downing three cups of java black, I'm headed back to the vineyard. Seems some kids in the wee hours of the morning decided to wreak havoc at the vineyard and one of them took a drive in one of the tractors."

"I don't like where this is going."

"Just wait. The kid apparently drove it right into the pond, jumped out before it sank, hit the bank on the side, and broke his arm."

"You're kidding."

"Nope." Derek sighed. "The worst part is, the mother is screaming the words 'lawyer' and 'sue' at poor Manuel."

"They can't do that."

"In this litigious society who knows what they can do. Let's hope not. Anyway, see why I had to take a drive back and get this handled? Why don't we have dinner tomorrow night? Sound good?"

"It does. Seven?"

"Seven it is. I'll be by. I don't know if I'll see you around the winery or not. I've got some business to take care of outside the winery, plus Tara Beckenroe is doing an interview with me for *Winemaker Magazine*."

"Oh."

"I'm not too happy about it either, but since Gabriel's death, wine sales have dropped some. I need to do some public relations, and it's a good trade magazine to do it in. Believe me, she is the last person I want to have lunch with."

He was having lunch with Tara? An uneasy feeling settled in Nikki's stomach. She knew it shouldn't. Tara was who she was, and Derek was smart enough to see right through her. For some reason that didn't make her feel any better.

They hung up the phone after a few more minutes of chitchat and with Nikki reassuring Derek that she'd make it home with Simon and Marco, as those were her original plans anyway.

The drive home was glum and somber as Marco drove with Simon suffering a massive headache, a black eye, and a major bruise to his ego.

Nikki didn't mind the silence; it gave her time to think about the weekend and make plans for what she needed to do next. In her head she ran down everything she had learned. Susan and Jennifer didn't come from Rockefeller lineage. Jennifer herself had been recently placed in the will and looked to have the most to gain financially from Susan's death, besides Kristof.

Then there was Paulo. As much of a jerk as he appeared to be, he made good points about why he wouldn't have wanted Susan dead. Weren't his exact words "why murder the best lay I ever had?" Maybe, he murdered her for something else. Maybe he was actually jealous of her new husband. Nikki recalled the anger in his eyes on the day of the wedding. He didn't look like a happy camper. Could he be one hell of an actor? Sure it didn't bother him to have all sorts of women hanging on the line waiting their turn, but he could've been lying to her when he'd said that it didn't bother him that Susan had other men.

Then, there was good and drunk Blake Sorgensen, who'd conveniently left the reception early for Mexico for a few days. The strange thing about him was that Nikki did believe that he'd loved Susan. Man, did that girl get around, which made Nikki wonder for a second if Kristof hadn't murdered his new wife. A thought she'd have to come back to, because for now, she was only trying to categorize those people who she knew might have possible motives, and those she knew for sure were in San Francisco over the weekend. She hadn't forgotten the very important fact that whoever had tried to run her down and scare her away from the truth had also lived in or been visiting the city where Tony Bennett left his heart.

Blake had admitted his love affair with the much younger woman, who not only broke his heart, but worked hard at sucking him dry. And her lame excuse for leaving him in the dust was so she could marry a younger man whom she could have children with, which according to Deirdre Dupree was not really in Susan's plan at all. Or at least, if there were going to be children at the Waltman Castle, Susan had no plans of playing June Cleaver. Could Blake have been so torn up by Susan's admitted change of heart that he'd done away with her? Was drowning in alcohol a guise to rid himself of the memory of murdering a woman he once claimed to love? Could be.

All of it could be. The one thing Nikki knew could not be was that Isabel killed Susan. Someone else had done that and framed Isabel for it. Nikki dug out the pictures of Isabel and Kristof from her purse and thumbed through them one more time. Someone had been watching them. Her guess was it had been Susan herself. Susan certainly didn't kill herself, though. Then there was Louis, the waiter gone missing. Yikes. Now he could have possibly followed Nikki and tracked her to San Fran in an attempt to get her off the trail. But that really didn't seem plausible to her—it was too far-fetched.

These thoughts ran through her head, until she finally closed her eyes, weary from thinking too much. She drifted off to sleep, relaxed by the gentle sway of the powerful car.

When she opened her eyes, Marco was pulling up in front of her place. Simon was out cold, snoring. Nikki whispered a "thank you" to her newfound friend and accomplice, then watched him drive on up the hill toward the estate mansion.

After getting inside and setting her bag down, she headed straight for her computer in the arched alcove in her kitchen. She hooked up to the Internet and went to work.

There was one more thing bothering Nikki and it had to do with Pamela. Pamela didn't appear to come from the same mold as Susan. What had made the friendship what it was? From all accounts Pamela had really been in love with Antoine Ferrino. Money was not a factor from what everyone who knew them together had said. Why would Pamela sustain a friendship with Susan for as many years as they had? Granted Susan fronted herself for Kristof and others, but Pamela didn't seem to be under any pretense where her friend was concerned. It nagged Nikki a bit. They just didn't fit, other than that they were both gorgeous. Nikki had to wonder if Pamela's love for Antoine was real, and now Marty. So what, though? How would that weigh into murdering Susan? It really didn't. What did weigh in for Nikki was this whole underlying question that had kind of been plaguing her since the wedding, and meeting the people she had in the last week, Daveed and Angel included. Could true love reign between a young beauty and an old beast?

Her curiosity was getting to her in regard to this age-old question. She made one more trip through the search engine on the Internet and found the names of Pamela's stepchildren. How she would approach them she wasn't sure. She wasn't even sure why she should bother calling them. She didn't think that anything they said would lead her to discovering who had killed Susan. The thought she kept trying to push aside came to her mind. Was it possible that Isabel did murder Susan? She refused to believe it as guilt consumed her for even thinking of it. Tears sprang to her eyes at the mere frustration of it all. Crying wouldn't help Isabel. She wiped them away as she hardened her resolve to see her friend out of the awful predicament she was in.

Chapter 24

Nikki came up with a story to tell Carmen Ferrino Spencer.

"Who did you say you were again?" Carmen asked.

"I'm Mickey Strands." Oh, God, what a stupid name, but it came to her in that instant that it might be better to use a fake name, and that was what came to her. "I do some freelance writing for various women's magazines. I'm currently writing an article on true love and how it can defeat all obstacles."

"Okay." Carmen sounded skeptical. "Why are you calling me, then? Stan and I love each other, but you know we aren't any different than the average couple. Who gave you our number?"

"Actually I'm calling to speak with you about your father Antoine and his marriage with Pamela Leiland. I got your number from a friend of theirs who said they had a great marriage. The kind that was against all odds."

"My father died last year."

"I know. I'm terribly sorry. I've heard wonderful things about your dad and how gracious he was. I've also heard how wonderful he and Pamela were together and how much in love they were."

"Have you spoken with Pamela?"

"I have not. I did call her, but I spoke with someone, I can't remember who now, who informed me that Pamela recently lost a dear friend of hers and wasn't up to talking with anyone currently. I was told to try back in a week or two. Did you know about that?"

"Yeah, her kooky friend Susan. Pamela actually called me the other night after it happened and told me about it. She was pretty shaken up."

"I can imagine. From what I'd heard they were like sisters."

"I never got that about Pamela and Susan. I mean we all tolerated Susan, especially my dad. She was not the nicest woman you'd ever meet. Nothing against her. I hope she rests in peace, but she wasn't too pleasant. But Pamela liked her and they were friends from way back, you know. Susan did seem to treat Pamela nicely. They did a lot of stuff together. I was even kind of jealous of their friendship."

"Really? Why?"

"Because Pamela and I were really close, too."

"So, you liked her and supported her relationship with your father?"

"Totally. At first I wasn't too keen on her. You've probably seen her a few years back in some print ads, but she didn't make it as the top model she wanted to be. Of course, I thought when she met and married my dad that it was all for the money."

"You changed your mind?"

"I did. My dad had some rough times and Pamela stood by him. She didn't care. I even overheard an argument between her and Susan about it. Susan was urging her to leave my dad. I think the words she said were something like, 'move on to greener pastures. Find someone worth it. Someone with deep pockets.' Pamela told her to back off. That she loved my dad and wasn't about to leave him."

"What did this Susan gal say to that?" Nikki hoped she'd keep talking and not catch on to the true quest of her phone call.

"Nothing, because I walked in at about that time. Susan shut her big mouth right away."

"It really was true love then, between your dad and Pamela?"

"Definitely. She was torn up when he died. Really torn up. Susan kind of drifted out of Pamela's life after that argument I overheard, but came bouncing back into her life after my dad was gone and insisted that Pamela move in with her. Kind of weird. Pamela and I lost touch for a little bit. I guess we each had to mourn in our own way."

"You said she called you a few days ago though."

"She did. We've rekindled our friendship. In fact, about a month ago when she was in the city she stopped by my husband's business, that's where I work, too. She wanted to take a look around because we're expanding. We're branching out around the country. She hung out for a bit and took a tour of the place. Then we went to lunch."

"That's wonderful that you've remained good friends. What do you and your husband do, can I ask?"

"It's nothing glamorous, I can assure you. But we make good money because everyone needs one."

"Needs one, what?"

"An exterminator. We have a chain of pest control companies."

"Like insects, rodents?"

"You got it. That's what we do. See, nothing exciting."

Nikki heard a baby wail in the background.

"Sorry, I gotta go. Hope I helped. Trust me, my dad and Pamela truly loved each other. Bye."

Nikki set the receiver down and went on another search. She knew that what had killed Susan had been poison, but now the weapon of choice had opened up a whole handful of possibilities. More than ever before.

She typed in the poison's name that was used to kill Susan—Sodium Fluoroacetate. Right there in black and white was the fact that Sodium Fluoroacetate was a poison used in killing rodents. Nikki knew that if she were to confirm her suspicions she'd have to wait and call back to Carmen's husband's company in the morning when they opened. Then she'd have to make a visit to the Waltman Castle.

She tossed and turned all night long, running various scenarios through her mind. By the time Monday morning rolled around she'd been up half the night. At eight o'clock she called The Spencer Pesticide Co., and got her answer.

"Yes, I need to have my house treated. I have a nest of rats in the walls. I was wondering if you use Sodium Fluoroacetate?"

"Yes, ma'am, we do. We're very careful with it, however, and we can assure you that it will get rid of your problem."

"That's wonderful," Nikki replied. "Oh, I'm sorry. I'll have to call you back. My husband just walked in the room, and I need to tell him something before he leaves for work. Thanks."

Nikki turned off the phone. *Husband?* The invisible one with the good looks, smart brain, sense of humor, and ability to make a woman scream with pleasure. And where was he? Maybe in his house across the pond from her. She knew for a fact that Derek was all of those things, except for the pleasure screaming part, and something told her he probably had a handle on that, too.

Sodium Fluoroacetate was the poison that killed Susan. Nikki had read that it was odorless and tasteless and could kill a person in a matter of minutes to an hour. Susan must've had quite a bit to have it work as quickly as it did, because if it had taken longer than minutes, then the symptoms of nausea, nosebleeding, and vomiting would have shown up. She'd snorted it from a vial because she thought it was cocaine.

Pamela had been inside her former stepdaughter's place of business only a month earlier where the poison was kept on hand. Now that Nikki *thought* she knew who the killer was, she would have to get the proof she needed in order to see that Isabel was released from jail and the right person placed behind bars.

She would have to call Kristof once she got into her office. Once there, she was surprised that a rep from the Waltman Castle had already left her a voice mail—Deirdre Dupree.

"Hi, Nikki. There's a note here on my desk to give you a call about the grapes we discussed the other day. Marty wants to see you this afternoon at around four, if that works. I can't make it, though. I have another appointment. Sorry. Can you call me back and leave a message? I'll be out a good share of the day. Oh, and it says here that he'd like you to come by the house instead of the winery. Thanks."

Lady Luck was on her side. She'd go and see Marty about the grapes and then talk to Kristof about what she believed was the truth. He'd have to listen to her. She believed there was a part of him that cared about Isabel, and although she'd considered him a viable suspect, especially after spotting him with Deirdre the other day, she didn't think he had it in him. He was a womanizer, not a killer.

Once Nikki presented to him everything she'd found out, then he could go to the police and they would reopen the investigation. Hopefully. She returned Deirdre's call and left her a voicemail confirming the four o'clock appointment with Marty.

The day dragged on, as she formed multiple conversations in her head with Kristof and how it might all go.

Nikki checked her watch and the clock several times throughout the day. It was finally time to close up shop and head out. She said her goodbyes to her co-workers and got behind the wheel of her car.

On the drive over, she decided to call Simon and Marco, give them a run down of her findings. She hadn't seen them around all day and figured they must still be trying to work out their differences. Since being back at the vineyard they'd popped their head inside her office at least once a day to show her either some new sketch or idea on their Zen Wine Campaign, or to provide her with more wisdom from the Guru Sansibaba. She got their voice mail and left them a message on Marco's cell.

She made it to Sonoma in record time even with the traffic. She chided herself for not keeping within speed limits. Highway 12 was not a highway anyone should be speeding on, but she wanted to get this over with. Her plan was to talk honestly with Kristof about everything she'd found out. He might or might not believe her. She doubted the police would, so she'd thought that out of everyone in this group of dysfunctionals, Kristof might be the one who could be open and rational.

Nikki pulled up in front of the Waltman Castle in all it's grey brick and slate glory at around four o'clock. Standing at the front door, Nikki began to feel uneasy. She hadn't thought this through enough, and the knot in the pit of her stomach told her it was a bad idea. She'd arrange a different meeting time with Marty in regard to the grapes. She started to turn and head back down the stairs, when the front door opened. There stood Pamela.

"Hey, Nikki. Come on in. Marty said that you were popping by."

Nikki entered the house, and Pamela closed the door behind her.

"Follow me. I'll pour us a glass of wine."

"Sure. Sounds good." Nikki followed Pamela with trepidation because she was pretty certain she was walking in the footsteps of a murderer. However, placating a killer, instead of letting on to what she knew, was probably the smartest move. She didn't want Pamela to have a clue that she was on to her.

"I'll be right back with our wine. Make yourself comfortable." Pamela motioned to the living room chair.

Nikki took a seat and watched as the tall brunette sashayed into the kitchen. She was all glamoured out in black silk pants and a white silk wrap shirt. A bit chichi for the daytime, but whatever.

It would be a few moments before Pamela returned and Nikki's mind and stomach churned. She glanced up at that portrait of old Ben Waltman and shivered. Why was it that stupid portrait gave her the creeps, maybe even more so than Pamela? Damn, if it didn't look like something out of an old movie where the eyes were real and watching every move she made. Nikki turned away from it and looked down the hall that led to the kitchen.

What if Pamela did know that she was on to her? Where was Marty? Kristof? Sara? Nikki got the feeling that she was going to have to think fast on her feet. Pamela came back in and set down her wine in front of her. Nikki made

sure that before she made her next strategic move that
Pamela, too, sat down, took a sip of her wine and started to
get comfortable.

Nikki then asked, "Where's Marty? He knew I was
coming by. He had Deirdre leave me a message."

"I know. I was actually the one who relayed the message
from Marty to Deirdre to phone you. He should be here
any minute. He had a luncheon and meeting that ran late
over at the winery. Kristof is with him, I believe."

"What about Sara? Doesn't she usually join you for
your evening glass of wine?"

"She does. But she was feeling tired today, and I believe
she is out in the guest house napping."

"Getting old doesn't sound fun." What else was she supposed to say to the killer in the room, one who she was alone
with? "I'd really love some cheese and crackers with this. I
don't mean to be a pest. It's just that I skipped lunch today."

"I don't mind at all." Pamela stood and walked out of
the room.

Thankfully she didn't take her wineglass with her.
Maybe this could all work in Nikki's favor, if Pamela was
on to her, then it might be easier to catch her than she
thought.

When Pamela came back she set down a tray of cheese
and crackers in front of Nikki. "I'm sorry, but could I use
the bathroom?"

Pamela gave her a quizzical look. "Of course. It's down
the hall and to your right."

"I remember. Thanks." Nikki tried to nonchalantly head
toward the bathroom, wineglass in hand. Once there she
closed and locked the bathroom door behind her and took a
breath. She then poured out half her glass of wine. After that
she dug through her purse and found what she was looking
for—a palette of MAC lipsticks and glosses that she'd

recently purchased. One of the colors would work perfectly. She didn't want to touch the rim of the glass with her lips. But she knew for this to work, she'd have to. She first found some wet wipes that she liked to carry with her, also in her purse. She wiped the rim of the glass and then dried it. She applied the lipstick to her own lips, made an imprint on the glass, and then removed the lipstick, that was way too dark for her, from her lips.

A light breeze seemed to pass by her and she spun around. No one was there. This place was definitely high up on the freaky meter. She rubbed her arms to get rid of the goose bumps that had popped out on them. Cursing under her breath, she said, "If that's you, Mr. Waltman, I know that you weren't your granddaughter's favorite relative, but I'm asking you, if I'm in the company of a murderess, could you please help me out? And, if you do, I promise, I'll do what I can to help you go to the Light or at least convince your granddaughter that maybe you weren't such a bad guy after all. Please." Wow, did she feel stupid talking to someone who she knew wasn't there, and even though she believed in ghosts, the way Sara Waltman referred to her grandfather as an old bastard, she had her doubts that he'd help her get out of this predicament. All this talk from the boys about Guru Sansibaba even had her telling some bastard ghost who probably didn't exist that she'd help him into the Light. She was definitely losing it.

There was not time to embark on spiritual enlightenment or to go insane at the moment, so she went forward with her plan to catch the killer and reapplied her own light colored lipstick, flushed the toilet for effect, then washed her hands. Before leaving the bathroom she pressed 'record' on her compact recorder. She'd slipped it into her purse before leaving her office. She didn't know at the time if she could trust Kristof Waltman or anyone who lived in the castle, for that matter. It had been a thing for assurance and now she was pleased with herself for being so distrustful.

Returning the running tape recorder back into her purse, and glass in hand, she crossed her fingers and hoped she was about to get more than what she'd initially come here for.

Upon returning to the living room, she noticed that Pamela was staring out the large windows looking rather pensive. She turned back to Nikki and smiled. "I take it you're here to see Marty about some of our wines?"

Hmmm. Our wines? "I'm tying up some loose ends on a deal we're making with the Waltmans to buy some cabarnet grapes from them. From the looks and sound of it, you'll be getting involved in the wine business yourself. You seem to be fitting in nicely here."

Pamela sipped her wine. Nikki set her glass down on the side table next to her.

"It's a strange thing. My friend falls for Kristof, then is killed, and in the meantime I fall in love with Marty. It didn't work out for Susan and I'm still very distressed over that, but it is working out better for me."

"That's wonderful. Are wedding bells in the future here at the castle?"

She laughed and flipped her long, slicked-back ponytail. "Not here. Not with the curse I think that's on this place. I really do think that Ben Waltman haunts this castle, and if I have my way, Marty would tear it down and start fresh. I can't ever shake the feeling that I'm being watched. No, when Marty and I get married, we'll probably go somewhere tropical and secluded. I'm not like Susan was. I don't need an ostentatious wedding."

"I know what you mean." Nikki took another look up at the portrait on the wall. She looked back at Pamela, who seemed to be studying her in a way that made her start fidgeting with her earring—a nervous tic she had when uncomfortable around others, and she was most uncomfortable around Pamela Leiland at that moment. "I take it that you've moved in here? Have you been able to retrieve all of your things in San Francisco? I know that you were sharing a townhome there with Susan."

Pamela smiled again at her, although this time there was a sardonic edge to the smile, and Nikki felt a sliver of fear snake down her back "Actually, I was in the city over the weekend and got the rest of my things."

Nikki swallowed hard. It was coming together now. "No kidding? I was, too. If I'd known, we could've gotten together."

Pamela nodded slowly, her eyes still trained on her, half closed into slits. "How do you like your wine?" Pamela tilted her head to one side and took a sip of her own glass of wine.

"It's very good. But I'm actually not feeling too well all of a sudden." Nikki leaned her head back onto the sofa's back.

"That's too bad. Maybe you should finish the wine."

"I feel kind of dizzy and sick to my stomach."

Pamela stood and walked over next to her and sat down, placing a hand on her shoulder. "Yes. I bet you do, and in a few moments your nose may start to bleed, you might even vomit, and then all of your organs will start to boil one by one, and there will be nothing that can save you."

"What are you talking about?" Nikki moaned, and hoped her acting was better than when she'd been on her short-lived cop show.

"You should've stuck with wines, my friend. I had no beef with you, and it was all working out perfect for me, until you went and started snooping around."

"What? I don't understand," Nikki groaned. She tried to sound weakened and desperate. "Help me."

"Can't do that. I killed Susan the same way I'm killing you, with a little drug the EPA isn't too fond of, but pesticide companies love it. Carmen and I are still pretty good friends. She called me last night to tell me that some woman had called and was doing a story on me and Antoine. I told her I hadn't heard anything about it. She said that the woman's name was Mickey Strands. Now, Nikki you're a smart lady. C'mon, Mickey Strands?"

Nikki knew she should've picked a better name.

"But even if you'd told Carmen that your name was Veronica Higgins, I would've known it was you because you're the only one who has been so damn nosey."

Nikki slid to the floor and rolled on her side.

"Here I thought that maybe you had the brains to back off, after I warned you in the city to mind your own business. I really didn't want to have to hurt you. I think you're a nice woman.

"The bad thing for me, when I found out what you've been up to, is that I had to make it so someone else could take the fall. The good thing for you, at least, is that you'll get what you've been wanting all along."

"You're insane," Nikki whispered. "What are you talking about?"

"Your friend Isabel will go free, because although I've had to work harder than a dresser backstage at a fashion show to pull this thing off, I've made it now where actually the perfect murderer is that old bag asleep in the guesthouse. I figure it won't matter too much if they lock her away. She's only got a couple of years left, if that. But you've met her. Her mind is sharp and she could've done this as easily as I have."

Nikki coughed and gagged, keeping her attacker still in belief mode that her plan was working out.

"There's not time for me to explain that now, because in

about six minutes you should be dead, and since these are your last minutes I feel like I owe you an explanation. You've worked so hard to figure this mystery out. I'm surprised that the Sodium Fluoroacetate is working so quickly on you. I'd given most of it to Susan and only had a little of it left. I'd planned to get rid of it, but now I'm glad I didn't. The sooner it works for you, the better it is for everyone. Get this whole thing over with."

"Please help me." Nikki turned over and stared up at Pamela. She'd made herself drool, and rolled her eyes back into her head. Look out Nicole Kidman. Was there an Oscar in Nikki's future?

"Sorry. You know I can't do that." Pamela patted her shoulder as if they were friends. "I killed Susan because she took away what was precious to me. I was only returning the favor. You see, Susan was everything you thought she was, and what most people thought she was. She was greedy, manipulative and power hungry. She used people. For a while I thought she was onto something. I enjoyed our games of hooking rich men and taking them for all they were worth. Then I met Antoine, and it was supposed to be like the rest. We got married and Susan devised a plan to murder him once I was in the will. What Susan didn't expect was for me to fall in love with him, his kids, everything about him. He was a good, loving, sweet man, and the money didn't matter, because he wasn't good with it, and he wasn't worth all that much when he passed away."

Nikki moaned and grabbed her stomach.

"I told Susan that there would be no murder. Nothing. That I loved Antoine and we were going to have a baby. But Susan wasn't about to let that happen. She was jealous and she liked things the way they used to be, and she murdered him. I couldn't prove it. She wouldn't admit it to me, until one afternoon over lunch here in the valley. After I got her juiced up on a few bottles of champagne, I pointedly asked her if she had killed him. I told her I wouldn't be upset but that I needed to know. I lied and told her that I was stupid to ever think I loved Antoine and was especially angry that he left me with nothing. I told her that I was grateful to her for taking me in after he died. What she didn't know was I had gone to her after he died always hoping to find the truth.

"That day she told me. She admitted to slipping amphetamines into his heart medication, which shot his blood pressure up and caused his heart to fail. She had caused his death, and I had my proof, so I could get my revenge. I knew I had a fall gal in Isabel. I figured Kristof and Susan were two peas in a pod, getting sex when and wherever, off of the pretty people that they could. I started following Kristof around, and I saw him several times with Isabel. I never told Susan what I knew. I only told her about Grapes and Isabel and how I thought they would be better caterers for her than Domaine Chandon—you know, new and up and coming, were the words I think I used, and it worked. Susan made Isabel an enemy on her own, because she loved to jerk the little people around, and it worked out perfectly for me. What was even better was I found out that Isabel had her own stint at partying, and knowing that Susan liked to do blow once in awhile, I put the poison in a vial. Remember, the bridesmaids wore long gloves that day. I gave Susan the vial on her way to the changing room and told her to have a wild time on her big day. Instead of cocaine, she snorted the poison through her nose. I whispered in one of the caterer's ears that I'd heard someone had cocaine and that the bride was looking for it. I knew that gossip would travel through the kitchen and of course, would be exaggerated and changed to make the story sound better, by the time the police got a hold of it."

"That's evil," Nikki whispered and gagged in between the words.

"Shh. Save your energy. I need to explain. Prior to that, I watched as the caterers drove in that day, and found the truck Isabel was driving. I took Isabel's sweater from her and offered to hang it up. The day after the party, I drove down to the truck rental place. I had written down the license plate number off of the truck Isabel had driven the day of the wedding. I waited for a bit until the guys working the counter were busy and distracted. Then, I got into the back room, and located the key to that truck easily enough, because they were numbered. After that, I got into the truck, planted Isabella's sweater and left.

"And, you know, it would've all worked out fine. Lucky for me, I found out you were in the city. It was a coincidence, but one that worked in my favor. Marty had appointments out here through the weekend, so I figured it would be a good time to grab the rest of my things from the apartment. I didn't bother telling Jennifer I was coming. I still have a key. When I went to retrieve my things from the condo, I saw you leaving. I hid and then I started following you. I tried to warn you, but you're a stubborn woman."

Nikki sat up and widened her eyes. She got to her feet. "I know I am, my aunt is always telling me so. You killed your best friend, because she killed your husband, and you framed my friend because it was easy, and now you're planning on framing Sara Waltman for my murder and Susan's. I have to ask, or should I suppose you were also the one to follow Susan and Blake and took those X-rated pictures you had sent to Sara Waltman. There is no private investigative team by the name of Lawson & Rennert. What you don't know is that I signed for those photos from the FedEx guy the day of the wedding. I assume you were hoping that if your frame-up of Isabel didn't work, then you could redirect the investigation to make it look as if Sara discovered Susan's seedier side and did away with her."

Pamela's jaw dropped.

"You know, for a time I started to wonder what it was that made you and Susan such pals; you seemed so nice, the opposite of her. Was I wrong, or what?" Nikki was right on that account—birds of a feather *do* flock together, and Susan and Pamela had been two of the same kind. Pamela may have loved Antoine, but she was a killer, exactly like Susan was.

Pamela stood, hands on hips. "What in the hell? You should be halfway to rigor mortis by now."

"Sorry." Nikki grabbed for her wineglass on the side table. "Would you look at that? I don't wear that shade of lipstick, but it looks like you do. Oops, I must've picked up your glass when you went to get the crackers and cheese. Sorry."

"What? Oh my God, Oh my God." Pamela wrapped her hands around her neck, and stood looking around as if something or someone in the room would save her.

Nikki laughed. "I figured you might try and poison me, too, since that's your modus operandi, but I fooled you."

Pamela screamed at her with a sound of rage, and lunged for Nikki, hitting her in the stomach. Nikki fell to the ground on her side. Pamela scrambled to her feet and started to come at Nikki with her hands at the ready to lock around Nikki's neck. Nikki reacted by hooking her leg around Pamela's and kicking her in the calf. Pamela stumbled. It gave Nikki enough time to stand up. She ducked her head low and dove straight for Pamela's gut, pushing her to the ground and knocking her down.

Pamela flailed her arms and hands, hitting Nikki repeatedly on the back. Pamela being the larger woman, she was able to roll them both onto their sides, and she did manage to get her hands wrapped around Nikki's neck. As Nikki struggled to remove Pamela's hands, she felt like she was beginning to lose consciousness, and a dismal thought crossed her mind that maybe Pamela would win. Then the voice of angels rang out.

"Marco, I don't think it's female mud wrestling. Get her." It was Simon.

Marco jumped on Pamela, and both he and Simon pulled her off of Nikki, and then pushed her away from her. Nikki sat up to catch her breath. Marco held Pamela's arms back behind her.

Pamela yelled at her. "You can't prove a damn thing other than we had a silly little catfight between us."

Nikki stood up and straightened herself. "That's where you're wrong." She reached for her purse and pulled out the tape recorder. "It's all right here." She waved the recorder in Pamela's face.

"Oh, no, you have to get me to a hospital. The poison."

"Oh, please. I lied. I wasn't sure if you'd put poison in the glass, but I wasn't going to take the chance." She then explained what she'd done to further elude Pamela's plans. "I'm not a killer. Even if you may not deserve to live, and a judge will determine that, I wouldn't murder anyone."

Nikki dialed the police on her cell phone.

They arrived and took Pamela into custody. Detective McCall stayed behind and questioned Nikki, along with the boys. As they were getting ready to leave, Marty and Kristof showed up, aghast at what had occurred in their absence.

Marty's face scrunched up in a look of despair. He'd been duped again. Nikki wondered if he'd fallen in love with Pamela. She felt sorry for him.

Kristof sat down at the bottom of the staircase, shaking his head. "I can't believe it. They were best friends."

"They were both murderers. Pamela murdered Susan for killing her husband, Antoine," Nikki said.

"Is that what Pamela told you? That Susan killed Antoine?" he asked.

"That's what she claims."

"That's preposterous. I can't believe any of this. I am happy though to know that it wasn't Isabel who murdered Susan. I never thought her capable of doing such a thing," Kristof said.

"It might have been decent of you to let her know that when she was first arrested and accused, especially since you were so close not that long ago," Nikki replied.

Marty's head snapped around and he glared at Kristof. Oh yeah, little boy bad had some explaining to do to dear old dad.

A crew of investigators showed up to search through the castle. They woke Sara who came ambling in through the French doors off the patio that led to the guesthouse. "What the hell is going on here?" she asked, waving her cane in the air.

"It's okay, Auntie, they caught the real killer," Kristof said. "Isabel Fernandez didn't do it."

"The real killer? I'm not surprised that Miss Fernandez didn't kill that bimbo you married for about five minutes. Who did it? That other bimbo who was hanging around here? What's her name Martha? Marcy?"

"Pamela," Marty replied.

"Right. Dumb hussy, too. Who figured it out?" She looked at Nikki, and then pointed at her. "It was you, wasn't it? You're a smart cookie. I know."

Nikki nodded.

"How did you know, Auntie?" Kristof asked.

"I used to write mysteries, remember?" She smiled at Nikki who returned the smile.

Nikki remained baffled at how Sara Waltman had written a mystery similar to the real life one that had gone on.

Or at least there were the similar aspects. Nikki shrugged it off. After all, fact was stranger than fiction.

That thought running through her mind, she glanced at the portrait of Ben Waltman. The eyes didn't seem so life-like to her any longer.

"Old bastard," Sara said.

"What?" Nikki asked.

Sara pointed to the portrait with her cane. "He woke me up from my nap."

Everyone in the room was now looking at Sara.

"He did. Said that he was on his way to a better place, tired of watching over me and the rest of this family. Said we were all hopeless anyway. I told him good riddance, and that's when I came in here to see what the hell was going on."

"You were dreaming, Aunt Sara," Kristof said. "Great Grandpa does not haunt this place."

At that moment the portrait on the wall slipped and tilted to the side. The room went silent for a minute. "Sure he doesn't," Sara replied. "You told me you were leaving, you old coot, now get on with it."

A light breeze traveled through the family room, and then the air settled into stillness. Sara winked at Nikki. Nikki said a silent "thank you" to Ben Waltman, not knowing whether or not he had had anything to do with helping her out that afternoon, but she certainly didn't want him haunting her, so a thank you was indeed in order. And, at that moment, so was a full glass of wine.

Chapter 25

"Red or white?" Nikki asked Isabel as she perused the wine selection at Grapes, while Isabel made dinner for herself, Nikki, and Andrés, who was, as usual, running late.

"Let's start with champagne," Isabel replied.

"Excellent idea," Nikki said. "Should we wait for Andrés?"

They simultaneously said, "Nah." Then laughed together.

"I missed that so much in this week that I never thought would end," Isabel said.

"What? Wine?"

"No. Laughing with you, and thinking same thoughts and having you here with me." Isabel set a tray of Gruyère toasts with caramelized onions and prosciutto in the oven. "And I have missed this." She glanced around her restaurant that she'd closed for the evening so they could have a peaceful dinner. The media had been hounding Isabel

since her release the day before, but Andrés had hired a
handful of security guards and the reporters were getting
the picture, although both women knew they'd be back.
They were probably busy doing research on Pamela and
talking with former lingerie models to get the *real* scoop
on Pamela Leiland. Or pestering Carmen Ferrino, which
Nikki truly hoped they weren't, but it was inevitable.
Carmen had nothing to do with helping Pamela murder
Susan.

Pamela knew when the police took her in and interro-
gated her that she was sunk. She copped to the entire thing,
plus it was on Nikki's handy dandy recorder. Pamela admitted that the day she'd visited Carmen at the pesticide
company she found a few moments alone in the warehouse
by claiming she needed to use the restroom. That's when
she was able to pocket the poison.

"And I have missed cooking, especially for people I
love."

"You must be talking about me," Andrés said, walking
through the front door. He came over to Isabel and wrapped
his arms around her. "I know I've seen you a million times
since yesterday, but I can't stop hugging you, 'Mana." He
kissed the top of her head.

Nikki wiped away happy tears. Andrés looked hot.
There was no other way to think it or say it. He had the life
spark back in his eyes and the smile on his face, and the
love he felt for his baby sister made him beautiful.

He let Isabel go and reached for Nikki, whom he pulled
into his arms. Ooh, and he smelled good, too. She had to
banish these thoughts. For goodness' sakes, Derek was finally expressing interest and seemed to be reciprocating
her feelings, and now she was lusting after the Latin lover.
If she didn't know herself better, she'd think she was a

sex-starved, love-starved, horny woman. Well, it *had* been a while. *Stop it.*

"Thanks for everything you did," Andrés said.

"No need to thank me. Now, we've waited for you to open this champagne." She pulled away from him and winked at Isabel as she picked up the bottle of champagne from the counter that she'd started to open right before he'd sauntered in.

"Certainly." He took the bottle from her hands, his fingers grazing hers. He popped the cork and poured a glass for her. He licked the remnants of bubbles spilling over the sides of the flute.

"Oh, boy, is it hot in here, or what?" Isabel fanned herself with her hands and grabbed a flute, shoving it in front of Andrés. He laughed and Nikki tried to ignore the comment.

Champagne poured, Andrés made a toast. "To Isabel and to freedom."

"To Isabel," Nikki said.

They clinked their glasses together and drank champagne late into the night, until they were all a bit too looped to do anything but walk to Isabel's house, where they crashed for the night.

When Nikki woke the next morning she was on the couch with Andrés arm wrapped around her. A vague memory of watching a romantic comedy came over her, and although they hadn't kissed—because Nikki was pretty sure she'd fallen asleep—she was also pretty sure they'd come close.

With both Andrés and Isabel still asleep, she quietly grabbed her things and walked back to the restaurant, where she got in her car and drove back to her place. She'd have to tell Andrés that there was no future for the two of them.

She was in love with Derek. *Wasn't she?* And they were having dinner together that night, and Nikki had a feeling that what was brewing between them was going to come to a head. Andrés was simply sweet and handsome and just a friend. Only a friend.

Gruyère Toasts with Prosciutto, Caramelized Onions, and Sherry with Simi Sonoma County Chardonnay

This is a simple dish to be enjoyed with the best of friends. Even though Nikki, Isabel, and Andrés chose to open champagne to celebrate Isabel's freedom, this appetizer also pairs well with a bottle of Simi Sonoma County Chardonnay. The fruit used in this Chardonnay comes from the Carneros and Sonoma's Russian River regions. This wine has a creamy, buttery texture enhanced with flavors of pineapple, toffee, pear, and a touch of cinnamon. It's aged in French oak, which gives it that big bold California Chardonnay flavor.

   ¼ cup extra-virgin olive oil
   4 large onions, thinly sliced
   ¼ cup fino sherry
   1½ tsp caraway seeds, lightly toasted
   Salt and pepper
   12 slices rye bread or French baguette (depending on
      personal taste)
   ½ cup whole-grain mustard
   10 oz Gruyère cheese, shredded.
   12-oz package of prosciutto

Heat 2 tbsp of olive oil in each of 2 large skillets. Add half of the onions to each skillet and cook over moderately low heat until nicely browned, stirring occasionally. Scrape all the onions into one skillet. Stir in the sherry and caraway seeds and cook until the sherry is completely absorbed, about 1 minute. Season with salt and pepper.

Preheat oven to 400°. Lightly spread 1 side of each slice of bread with the mustard and arrange on a large baking sheet. Top with the onions, cheese, and prosciutto. Season with pepper.

Bake the open-faced sandwiches for 6 minutes, or until the cheese is melted and the edges of the bread are toasted. Transfer the toasts to a cutting board and cut each into 4 triangles.

Chapter 26

For the last time that week, Nikki and Derek had taken a rain check on dinner and they were finally able to get it together. Nikki had avoided speaking with Andrés all day. She knew she'd played the tease and wasn't too happy with herself. She knew she'd have to call him in the morning and talk about the night before. Hopefully, he was on the same page as she was and would chalk up their cuddling to drunken antics.

"I can't believe we're finally having dinner sans interruptions from the boys or anyone else for that matter," Nikki said, shaking Andrés from her mind.

"Including your alter ego," Derek replied.

Nikki puckered her lips into a faux frown and scrunched her eyes into a look of mock devilishness. "You don't mean my evil twin, Nancy Drew?"

"Yeah, she's the one. Except I'd say you're the evil half. If I remember from the couple of Nancy Drew books I read, she was pretty sweet; and you? I'm not sure I'd call you sweet."

"Gee, thanks." She laughed and took a bite of her dinner, finishing it up. They were at the Glen Ellen Inn, which defined romance with its warm colors of peach, burgundy, and gold, all lit up by candlelight and the fireplace in the corner, next to where they were seated. "We're finally alone and I'm waiting with bated breath to hear what it is you wanted to talk to me about all week."

Before he answered her, Derek motioned for the waiter and ordered strawberry shortcake along with a dessert wine for both of them. "I like to celebrate with dessert."

"You're going to make me wait until they bring dessert, aren't you?"

He nodded, a sly grin and a glint in his baby blues. "You know it."

"Fine. I'm a patient woman." Minutes later their dessert arrived. Nikki took a bite. "Excellent. Now will you tell me?"

"I've decided to build a boutique hotel and spa at the vineyard. What do you think?" Derek asked.

Nikki set the fork back down on her plate. "A hotel and spa?"

"Mhhm." Derek brought a finger up to the side of her mouth, touching it gently. "You got a little whipped cream there."

The heat rose in Nikki, flowing through her body. "Thanks," she replied in a whisper.

"Yes. It was actually Simon and Marcos' idea, but I like it, and I think you're a natural to help out with this. You have great taste and I trust you."

"Wow. That sounds wonderful."

"I think so, too. We'll have about thirty rooms and the spa will be great. You know, with massages and luxury body treatments with warm grapeseed oils and soaking baths with the essence of grapes."

"Massages? That does sound good."

"It does, doesn't it?" Derek brought his wine glass up for a toast. Nikki watched as he set the glass back down. What was that look on his face? Melancholy? Frustration?

"Is something the matter?" she asked.

He shook his head. "No. I was thinking that I have a special bottle of wine in my cellar saved for a celebration."

"Oh, well, this is an excellent wine."

"It is." He nodded and smiled warmly at her. "Besides we can save that bottle for another special day." He sighed and glanced away for a second.

She wondered what weighed so heavily on his heart.

He looked over at her, taking his free hand and grasping hers with a slight squeeze. He again raised his glass to toast. "To the Malveaux Inn and Spa and great massages."

Chapter 27

A knock on Nikki's door catapulted her off the sofa. Was it Derek? It had to be. He'd left her so confused, especially after all the flirting over dinner and the build up from being with him in the city. How much more could a woman take? She opened it. There stood Andrés. He stormed in, a look of intensity on his face. He almost appeared dangerous, but Nikki knew better.

"We have to talk," he said.

"Okay. You're right, we do," she replied. She knew she should've called him earlier and laid it all out on the table.

He didn't give her a chance as he turned her around and put his hands on her shoulders. His dark hair falling in front of his eyes. He raked it out of the way and looked at her like she'd never seen him look before. There was heat in those eyes that made Nikki's heart race.

"I'm tired of this."

"Of what?"

"This game. This cat and mouse game between you and Derek, you and me. It's driving me crazy. You're driving me crazy."

"I, um, okay. You're right. I've been . . ."

Andrés placed a finger on her lips. "Shhh. Let me say what I came to say and maybe when I'm done things will be different between us.

Nikki was stunned and couldn't say a word even if she wanted to.

"I know you have this thing for Malveaux, but I also feel and believe that there is something between us."

She started to protest, but he shook his head. "Hear me out. If Derek is such a fool that he can't see that you're in love with him and act upon it, well, I'll be the fool in love with you, and hope you'll be foolish enough to fall in love with *me*."

With that he put his arms around her and pulled her close. He kissed her hard on her lips. The kiss turned into one of heated passion as a surge of electricity shot through her body. Andrés pulled away from her as she started to fully respond to him.

"You think about that and let me know." He turned around and walked out the door.

Nikki stood watching the closed door after him, her mind and body reeling in a state of confusion and nerves, high with a sexual intensity she hadn't felt in a very long time.

Chapter 28

After dropping Nikki back at her place, Derek wanted to kick himself. There was so much more he'd wanted to say to her tonight, to tell her how he really felt. He'd chickened out. Again. What was it about her? Her eyes, her hair, that smile, the way she made him laugh. She was the whole package and yet he couldn't tell her. He'd never felt so afraid in his life. She held something over him and dammit, he'd never been around a woman who made his heart race the way she did. The other night in the city, he'd wanted to tell her, kiss her, and then Marco and Simon and their troubles got in the way. Since then, it was like the cat got his tongue and clamped down on his feelings.

He flipped on the stereo and Marvin Gaye's "Let's Get It On," was playing. All right, the hell with it. He was going to do it. He was going to go over to her cottage right this minute and tell her everything about how he felt.

Derek went to the wine cellar and found the bottle of

wine he wanted to share with her that he'd told her about over dinner.

Five minutes later Derek stood outside Nikki's door with the wine in his hand. He knew this was right. He wanted to tell Nikki that his feelings for her were far stronger than just for an employee or for a friend. His feelings weren't nearly that simple, and he should've told her at dinner. The fact was he wanted to be close to her. To smell the gardenia scent that enveloped her body, to look into her green eyes, to see that smile that lit up his world every time he saw it.

He lifted his fist to rap on the door, his heart thumping hard against his chest, his nerves taking a stranglehold on every part of him. Something caught his eye from inside Nikki's house. He nearly dropped the bottle in his other hand. His heart almost stopped. How stupid could he be? There was Andrés, his arms around Nikki, and they were kissing. They were kissing passionately. Derek turned around and swallowed. He fought down any emotion, as he walked back home where he took the bottle of wine and slid it back into its place.

Chapter 29

Nikki lay awake for hours tossing and turning, willing sleep to help her escape from this madness. Life was bizarre, sad, funny, and so ironic. She didn't know what to think of Andrés' words and kiss that had surged through her like a bolt of lightning. She also didn't know what to think of Derek and his flirtations, and then the way he continually backed off. It was enough to drive a woman crazy.

Then there was the issue of that biological clock that had somehow started ticking recently. Maybe it was when she'd seen those little children with their parents at the hotel in the city, or maybe it was the fact that every time she saw a baby these days, she got all mushy inside. And Andrés wanted that. He desired a family, and God, how he could kiss. But she couldn't deny her feelings for Derek. No matter what, they were there bubbling over the surface and she wanted to flipping explode.

Maybe Andrés was right. Maybe she should take that chance with him. Derek certainly didn't seem to be all that interested, and she was sure she'd sent him the signals. One minute he was hot and the next minute he was cold. Andrés did seem to know exactly what he wanted, and that was her. Both men were maddening in their own way.

Nikki was at least thankful for the fact that her best friend was now home and in her own bed, free to let her life unfold. She turned on the clock radio on the nightstand. Sheryl Crow was singing "The First Cut Is the Deepest." When the singer got to the part about trying to love again, Nikki groaned and turned it off.

She started to drift off to sleep with so many questions still on her mind, one in particular kept playing out. Was it better to try and fall in love with a man she had simmering feelings for—a man she considered a dear friend? Or should she continue pining away for a friend she wished loved her in the way she loved him? There had to be an answer out there somewhere, but for that moment, sleep finally took precedence and would delay any answers to the questions on her mind and in her heart.

Strawberries & Cream Napoleon with Deerfield Ranch Gold, Late Harvest Dessert Wine

So, the question remains, will Nikki and Derek ever fall into each other's arms, or will Andrés be the one who holds the key to her heart?

No matter who the man of her dreams turns out to be, she can't go wrong with this sensual and simple dessert. It's full of berries and whipped cream! Karen Bertrand and her husband, Christian, the owners of the Glen Ellen Inn Restaurant and Cottages, were gracious enough to share this recipe. Karen also recommends pairing it with Deerfield Ranch 2000 Gold Late Harvest Dessert Wine. It's a full-bodied botrytis white wine, very rich and very sexy (think of the Marilyn Monroe of dessert wine.)

MERINGUE

4 egg whites
1½ cups of confectioners' sugar
1 tsp Framboise liqueur

Heat oven to 200°. Line baking sheet with baking paper. In electric mixer, beat egg whites until they form stiff peaks. Add confectioners' sugar slowly, and continue to beat for approximately 10 minutes, until firm. Gently fold in Framboise liqueur.

Using pastry bag, pipe mixture directly onto baking sheets into flat heart shapes. Bake 2 hours, until meringues are dry.

STRAWBERRY CREAM

> 1 cup mascarpone
> 7 oz heavy cream
> ¼ cup confectioners' sugar
> 1 tbsp Framboise liqueur
> Fresh strawberries, tossed in sugar

Combine all ingredients and whip until they fold into soft peaks.

Assembly

Place meringue on plate; top with dollop of strawberry cream, top with meringue; repeat with more strawberry cream and top with meringue. Garnish with fresh whipped cream; this is also delicious served with strawberry champagne:

Fill glass ¾ with champagne, add 1 oz Framboise liqueur, garnish with fresh strawberry and raspberry.